"I wish the kids' social worker didn't have a thing against single parents, but I can't be something I'm not."

"No guy in sight?" Adam asked.

Actually, a very tempting guy sat across the table from her right now, looking as if he was about to make a mad dash out of the restaurant. But there was no way she'd admit that, even if this had turned out to be a real date, which it clearly hadn't.

"No," Julie said, "I'm not dating anyone at the moment. But maybe I can convince Mrs. Kincaid that she's wrong about single parents. My dad was in the military and deployed a lot, so my mother pretty much raised me alone. And she was a great mom. We were really close."

As she lifted her glass to take another drink, Adam got to his feet and said, "Listen, I have to run, but a weird thought just crossed my mind."

At this point, she'd consider wild ideas.

"What if we get married?"

* * *

ROCKING CHAIR RODEO:
Cowboys—and true love—never go out of style!

Dear Reader,

I'm excited to recommend another Harlequin Special Edition book this month to encourage readers to discover these compelling contemporary romances. The heroes and heroines are dynamic and relatable, trying their best to resist their attraction to each other while resolving the conflict that keeps them apart. But the undeniable chemistry that simmers between them cannot be denied. These books will pull you in and take you on an emotional and satisfying journey. Each story ends with a marriage proposal or wedding—delivering the happily-ever-after, because the love and security of family is the ultimate promise of Special Edition.

Judy Duarte penned this month's recommendation. Her classic voice and knack for handling emotional tension have won her numerous awards and two RITA® Award nominations. And Judy really has a way with Western romances and handsome cowboys!

In *The Lawman's Convenient Family*, Adam is a confirmed bachelor who enjoys playing the field until he meets Julie Chapman, a pretty, soft-spoken music therapist who's seen more than enough anger and violence in her life. Julie loves books with happy endings and dreams of one day finding a gentle husband and creating a family in a peaceful, stable home. As physical attraction grows and mutual respect builds, Adam and Julie are forced to reevaluate what they really want out of life.

If you enjoy stories about marriages of convenience, you'll love *The Lawman's Convenient Family*!

All the best,

Paula Eaves Miller

The Lawman's Convenient Family

Judy Duarte

HARLEQUIN® SPECIAL EDITION

Recycling programs
for this product may
not exist in your area.

ISBN-13: 978-1-335-57361-2

The Lawman's Convenient Family

Copyright © 2018 by Judy Duarte

Printed in U.S.A.

Since 2002, *USA TODAY* bestselling author **Judy Duarte** has written over forty books for Harlequin Special Edition, earned two RITA® Award nominations, won two Maggie Awards and received a National Readers' Choice Award. When she's not cooped up in her writing cave, she enjoys traveling with her husband and spending quality time with her grandchildren. You can learn more about Judy and her books on her website, judyduarte.com, or at Facebook.com/judyduartenovelist.

Books by Judy Duarte

Harlequin Special Edition

Rocking Chair Rodeo

Roping in the Cowgirl
The Bronc Rider's Baby
A Cowboy Family Christmas
The Soldier's Twin Surprise

The Fortunes of Texas: All Fortune's Children

Wed by Fortune

The Fortunes of Texas: The Secret Fortunes

From Fortune to Family Man

The Fortunes of Texas: The Rulebreakers

No Ordinary Fortune

Brighton Valley Cowboys

The Boss, the Bride & the Baby
Having the Cowboy's Baby
The Cowboy's Double Trouble

Visit the Author Profile page
at Harlequin.com for more titles.

To the amazing women who bore my
precious grandchildren: Bree Colwell,
Myrlett Colwell, Sarah Colwell and Christy Jeffries.
You are the best mothers ever.
Thank you for the beautiful babies and kiddos.

Chapter One

Detective Adam Santiago never wore costumes, unless you counted a disguise for use when he went undercover or on a stakeout. Yet here he was, dressed up as Zorro and attending the Autumn Gala, a local charity event.

The guy at the Halloween store had tried to talk him into getting a fake rapier, but Adam had declined. The costume was kitschy enough—he didn't imagine he needed to add any props to complicate things.

He had, of course, gone with the black eye-mask, which was resting on the passenger seat. If he didn't wear the typical Zorro eyewear, people might think he was just wearing a ruffled shirt for no reason. Or maybe that he was a bullfighter.

And speaking of other people, there'd be plenty of local folks inside who'd be surprised to see him here, since his idea of fun parties tended toward the smaller variety, something like having a few beers with a couple of friends at his favorite sports bar. Or better yet, a romantic dinner date that ended with breakfast. But tonight's gala was an exception. Adam had actually gone so far as to pay a hundred dollars to attend the event that would benefit both of his favorite local Brighton Valley charities, the Rocking Chair Ranch and Kidville, a children's home.

When he'd first learned of the gala, he'd planned to make a generous donation and to tell the folks in charge that he had to work tonight. But he'd changed his mind when he'd heard that Lisa Dawson would be here. A mutual friend had shown him a picture of her, although the image was a bit blurry.

Adam didn't need help when it came to meeting women, but his friend Stan had been pretty convincing. *Lisa's* perfect *for you. She's a flight attendant, house sitter and part-time dog walker, which means she's away from home a lot. So she won't expect you to spend every free moment with her. She's also bright and fun to be around. And like you, she's a big* Star Wars *fan. More important, her life's goal isn't to get married and to drive around town in a minivan full of kids.* When he still hesitated, Stan added, *She's also a blonde—and I know you're partial to them.*

That's when Adam agreed to meet Lisa. Lately, he'd gotten a little tired of playing the field. He wouldn't mind settling down some, but he wasn't going to make a major commitment to anyone. He liked his freedom way too much, not to mention his privacy.

But from what he'd gathered, Lisa might actually like the idea of having a one-on-one relationship with some well-defined boundaries. So he'd decided to approach her at tonight's gala. He had no idea what she'd be wearing, but he figured he could find her in the crowd and introduce himself.

Who knew? Maybe they'd hit it off immediately. And if so, they might even cut out early. *Together.*

He parked his classic 1973 Ford Bronco under one of the streetlights and headed to the front entrance, yanking at his shirt, wishing the damn sleeves weren't so poofy. As he approached the main entry to the Wexler Grange Hall, the outside of which had been decked out with bales of straw, scarecrows and the usual Halloween decorations, he slipped on his half mask. Then he stepped inside and scanned the crowd. Even in costumes, he recognized a lot of the townspeople, but he was more interested in seeking out one petite blonde.

And there she was, packing a fake lightsaber on her hip and wearing a skimpy outfit befitting an intergalactic warrior princess. The black strips of fabric that made up her short skirt revealed plenty of skin, including a striking pair of shapely legs. Her hair was swept up in a prim twist, an interesting contrast to that sexy outfit.

She had her back to him, but it had to be Lisa. She was the only petite blonde here. And, apparently, the only Star Wars fan.

Before he could cross the room and lay a little *buenos dias* on her, he spotted Donna Hoffman, who was dressed as Mrs. Claus. Donna and her husband, Jim, were in charge of Kidville, the home for abused and neglected kids between the ages of five and twelve. Adam met the couple when he'd offered to mentor some of the older boys. After he'd given them his résumé and shared his background as well as his reason for wanting to work with the troubled youths, he'd added, *Who better to lead a kid in the right direction than a guy who grew up in a similar situation?*

The Hoffmans had agreed, and he'd been volunteering his time there ever since. It was cool knowing he had something to offer those kids. He just hadn't counted on getting something from them in return.

"Hey, Donna," Adam said, greeting the older woman with a smile. "Or should I call you Mrs. Claus?"

She gave him a warm hug, then took a moment to check out his costume. "Did you lose your sword, Zorro?"

"I don't have a concealed carry permit for it, so I left it at home," he joked. "Besides, this seems like a pretty tame party. I doubt I'll need to use it."

Donna laughed and handed him a candy cane from the white frilly apron she wore over a red flannel skirt. "Jim and I bought our costumes for the Kidville Christmas party. I know they're not very Halloween-y, but rather than invest in something else for tonight, we decided to utilize them twice this year."

"Good idea." Adam's gaze drifted across the room, seeking Lisa—at least, he thought it was her. Who else could it be?

He spotted her near the buffet table, her back still to him, her hands on her hips. What was she doing?

And when was she going to turn around so he could get a glimpse at her face?

The party had barely begun, yet Lisa's appeal and his interest in her were growing steadily. He wondered what she had planned for the rest of the evening.

"Will you be coming out to Kidville again on Monday?" Donna asked, drawing him back to the here and now.

"You bet. I'm making some headway with Tommy."

"We've noticed. And so has his teacher. We all appreciate what you've done for him—the private tour of police headquarters, the ride-along in a patrol car, the visit to the ice cream shop afterward. Tommy's never had anyone take a special interest in him."

"Sometimes, that's all it takes." At least, that's how it had worked for Adam. Stan, his mentor, had been a cop, too. A patrolman who'd found him hanging out in the city park one night after curfew. A guy who'd eventually become his foster dad and his best friend.

Adam again glanced to the buffet table where he'd last seen Lisa, when Donna tugged at his poofy sleeve. "You keep looking across the room. What, or rather who, has caught your eye?"

Donna had been happily married for more than thirty-five years, and she thought everyone ought to take that same route, including Adam.

"I like looking at all the costumes," he lied.

"Aren't most of them great? It's amazing how some people go all out for an event like this."

He agreed, although it was one particular outfit that had caught his eye. He was just about to excuse himself and head for the buffet table when he glanced that way again and realized Lisa was no longer there. He took another scan of the room, including the dance floor, but she seemed to have vanished.

Maybe she'd gone to powder her nose—or whatever it was that sexy space women did.

What the hell? The night was still young. He'd find time to talk to her. And now that he'd seen her outside of her blurry photo, meeting her in person had become a high priority.

The food hadn't been brought out yet, but Julie Chapman didn't like the way the buffet table had been set up in the local Grange Hall. Before changing things around, she returned to the kitchen and asked Ralph Graystone, her boss and the owner of Silver Spoon Catering, if she had his permission to do so.

"Go ahead," Ralph told her as he filled a platter with appetizers. "You did a great job on the decorations at that wedding we catered last weekend, so I trust your judgment."

Julie thanked him, then returned to the party, stopping in the doorway long enough to tug at one of the flimsy black strips that made up her short skirt, the length of which had obviously been altered.

When Ralph asked the crew to wear costumes for tonight's event, she'd objected at first, explaining that she didn't have anything to wear.

Borrow something, he'd told her. *It's a Halloween party. We're all dressing up. I'm going to wear my chef's hat, but I'm painting my face like the Joker. And don't forget it's a charitable event.*

And that was the only reason Julie had decided to be a good sport about it, but she wasn't the least bit happy about the *Star Wars* getup Carlene, her coworker, had loaned her this afternoon, saying, *You'll be a space princess. A sexy badass.*

Julie had expected to wear some kind of sci-fi getup, but she had no idea that Carlene had shortened and altered the intergalactic costume to the point that Julie would reveal way too much skin. Unfortunately, she'd waited until the last minute to pick it up, and by the time she tried it on, it was too late to find something else.

Carlene, who was dressed as a bawdy tavern wench, her double Ds practically pouring out of the low-cut bodice, didn't seem the least bit uneasy about the way she was dressed. But unlike Julie, Carlene ran with a wilder crowd.

Still, when she entered the Grange Hall kitchen earlier, she'd told Carlene that she'd brought her Silver Spoon Catering shirt and a pair of black slacks with her and suggested it as a more appropriate option.

Her friend had clucked her tongue. *Don't be a party pooper, Julie. We're all dressing up this evening. Just go with the theme and have fun.*

So here she was, trying to make the best of it. And from the bursts of laughter coming from the people mingling in small groups and from the smiles of those kicking up their heels on the dance floor, everyone in attendance seemed to be having a good time so far.

But that didn't make Julie feel better about the way she was dressed.

Still, she had a heart for children, as well as the elderly. In fact, if she hadn't been working at the gala, she would have gladly paid to attend.

As she added the finishing touch to the second of two buffet lines, she scanned the festive Grange Hall, which the gala committee had decorated with wispy ghosts, dangling bats and spiderwebs. Then she double-checked the dinner tables.

Silver Spoon Catering had provided the food at a discount. The generous donation to the cause had actually been her boss's attempt to promote his new business venture and to impress some of the wealthier people in the area.

As Julie noted the smiling attendees, she suspected Ralph's plan just might work. She took a moment to admire their costumes, some of which were pretty cool.

One in particular, a man dressed as Zorro, caught her eye once more. The dark-haired, olive-skinned hunk was wearing black slacks, a crisp white shirt opened at the collar and a half mask. It was a great outfit, especially for a hot guy who appeared to be in his late twenties or early thirties.

She'd first noticed him when he'd entered the Grange Hall with a confident stride, clearly sure of himself. Off and on, she'd studied him surreptitiously, wondering who he was and realizing that he sure seemed to know most of the people here.

There was something vibrant about him, something

alluring that drew her attention. So much so, that she continued to steal glances his way every chance she got.

She'd better be careful, though. She had work to do and a job she needed to keep, even if she considered it only temporary.

She'd no more than turned away from the buffet line when she spotted Santa Claus. She recognized him instantly. It was Jim Hoffman, the director of Kidville—and just the guy she'd hoped to meet. Now was her chance. So she approached the heavyset gentleman and said, "Excuse me, Mr. Hoffman. My name is Julie Chapman, and I'm a music therapist. I'd like to make an appointment to speak to you about a job at Kidville."

He brightened, his eyes twinkling just like jolly ol' St. Nick's. "My wife and I would love to incorporate music into our therapy program, but our funding is stretched to the limit right now, so I'm afraid we can't offer a paid position."

Julie actually needed a steady paycheck, which was why she'd gone to work for the catering company. But she could also use some experience to add to her resume, not to mention an opportunity to get a foot in the door at Kidville.

"I'd be willing to volunteer for the time being," she said.

"Now, that's an interesting proposition. Do you have any experience?"

"I graduated recently and, other than working with children during my internship, I haven't had a paid position yet. But I majored in music, play several instruments and sing in my church choir."

"I'd like to discuss this further and hear more about your thoughts on a music therapy program, but this isn't a good time for either of us. Can you come to Kidville on Monday morning? I'll give you a tour, and we'll talk more then."

"Awesome. I'll be there bright and early."

As Mr. Hoffman strode away like Santa on a mission, Julie tugged at her skirt again. Apparently, her outfit hadn't bothered the man in charge of Kidville, which was a relief. Another potential boss or some of her more conservative church friends might not have been so accepting.

Too bad she hadn't thought to smear on some clown makeup before getting out of her car this evening. That would have hid her face, especially the flush on her cheeks. Oh, well… She'd just have to keep a low profile.

As she turned toward the kitchen, a tear-streaked redhead wearing a tiara and a long turquoise gown strode toward a pirate and let out a curse that made her sound more like a drunken longshoreman than the princess she was supposed to be.

She lifted her index finger and jabbed it at the pirate's chest. "I knew you were a big flirt, Derek, but do you have to be on the prowl when you're with me? I've had it with you. It's over for good this time." Then she removed her frilly white half mask, as well as her faux tiara, threw both on the floor and swept toward the entrance in a huff, leaving the frowning pirate in her wake.

Julie assumed he'd hurry after her. Instead, he let out a little chuckle and returned to the party.

You clearly made a wise decision, your majesty. And one you probably should have made sooner. Julie snatched the discarded white half mask from the floor, slipped it on her face and muttered, "Finders, keepers."

The moment she reentered the party, she spotted Zorro again, and her heart made a series of somersaults that would make a young gymnast proud.

She took a moment to appreciate his costume, not to mention his muscular physique and sexy swagger. Her interest, as well as her curiosity, grew by leaps and bounds. Who was he? Did he have a connection to Kidville or to the Rocking Chair Ranch?

She supposed it didn't really matter, so she did her best to shake off her attraction as she crossed the room. Before she reached the kitchen, a hand settled on her shoulder, warming her from the inside out.

She turned to see Zorro, his gaze locked on hers. When he offered her a dazzling smile, her breath caught.

"Lisa," he said, "I'd heard you were going to be here."

He clearly thought she was someone else. She probably ought to say something, but up close, the gorgeous bandito seemed to have stolen both her thoughts and her words.

"It's nice to finally meet you." His voice, whether authentic or altered to complement his costume, was laced with a slight Hispanic accent that set her senses reeling. "I've never really liked blind dates."

Talk about masquerades and mistaken identities. Before Julie could set him straight, he took her hand in a polished, gentlemanly manner and kissed it. His warm breath lingered on her skin, setting off a bevy of butterflies in her tummy.

"Dance with me," he said.

Her lips parted, but for the life of her, she still couldn't speak, couldn't explain. And she darn sure couldn't object.

Zorro led her away from the buffet tables and to the dance floor. When he opened his arms, she again had the opportunity to tell him who she really was. But instead, she stepped into his embrace, allowing him to take the lead.

His alluring aftershave, something manly, taunted her. As she savored his scent, as well as the warmth of his muscular arms, her pulse soared. She leaned her head on his shoulder as they swayed to a sensual beat, their movements in perfect accord, as though they'd danced together a hundred times before.

Now would be a good time to tell him she wasn't Lisa, but she seemed to have fallen under a spell that grew stronger with every beat of the music. The moment turned surreal, like she'd stepped into a fairy tale with a handsome rogue.

Once again, she pondered revealing his mistake and telling him her name, but there'd be time enough to do that after the song ended. Then she'd return to the kitchen, slipping off like Cinderella. But instead of a glass slipper, she'd leave behind her momentary enchantment.

But several beats later, a cowboy tapped Zorro on the shoulder. "Pancho, I need you to come outside."

Zorro looked at him and frowned. "Can't you see I'm busy?"

The cowboy, whose outfit was so authentic he seemed to be the real deal, rolled his eyes.

Julie wished she could have worn her street clothes. Would now be a good time to admit that she wasn't an actual attendee but here to work at the gala?

"What's up?" Zorro asked.

The cowboy folded his arms across his chest and shifted his weight to one hip. "Someone just broke into my pickup."

Zorro stiffened. "Right now? Where?"

"Here, in the parking lot. I had an envelope filled with cash donations to Kidville under the seat."

At that, Julie's heart thumped, and she clamped her mouth shut. Someone had stolen money meant for the Hoffmans' kids? Who would do such a thing?

"Is the money gone?" Zorro asked the cowboy.

"I don't know yet. I didn't look."

Zorro stiffened. "Any witnesses?"

"A stray dog. But he ain't talking."

"Very funny." Zorro's gaze returned to Julie. "I'm sorry, Lisa. I'm going to have to morph into cop mode."

Now it was Julie's turn to tense. He was actually a police officer in real life? A slight uneasiness settled over her, an old habit she apparently hadn't outgrown. Not that she had any real reason to fear anyone in law enforcement nowadays.

When Zorro removed his mask, revealing the rest of

his face, he was even more handsome than she'd imagined him to be. She stood mesmerized, darn near smitten by a face and persona that were movie-star quality.

The cowboy, who'd been frowning when he'd approached, wasn't bad looking, either. He tipped his hat to Julie. "Would you mind excusing us, ma'am?"

"No, not at all." Julie took a step back and glanced at Zorro.

A smile dimpled his cheeks, and little gold flecks in expressive brown eyes sparkled as he handed his mask to her. "Hold this for me. I'll be back."

She probably should have corrected his mistake then and there, but for the life of her, she couldn't seem to utter a single word.

As Zorro followed the cowboy out the side door, Julie held on to his mask as if it were a glass slipper and studied him from behind. He was both gorgeous and charming. A dashing ladies' man, no doubt. She could tell by his self-assurance and flirtatious manner, both of which were interest-snatching and blood-stirring.

They also set off flashing red warning lights. If there was anything Julie avoided these days, it was suave and flirtatious men who thought they were God's gift to women.

And Zorro, the handsome devil, was too darn sexy to be heaven-sent.

Chapter Two

As Adam followed his old high school friend away from the dance floor, he glanced over his shoulder and took one last look at Lisa, regretting he'd have to put off getting to know her. At least he'd finally had a chance to meet her.

"I'm sorry I interrupted your dance," Matt said as they slipped out a side door and headed toward the parking lot.

"So am I. I've been waiting a long time to meet that woman, and after holding her in my arms and catching a whiff of her citrusy scent... Hell, I need to get back inside before someone else tries to take up where I left off."

"Hopefully, you can get to the bottom of that break-in quickly."

"If I can't, I'll call into headquarters and have someone on duty come out here." Adam needed to get back to that gala. And to Lisa.

The buddies crossed the graveled parking lot, their footsteps crunching on the pulverized granite. Unlike Adam, Matt didn't look any different tonight than he usually did. He was sporting a pair of new Tony Lama boots, though. And he had on a spiffy new Stetson, too. But that wasn't surprising. Costume parties weren't Matt's style.

And normally, they weren't Adam's, either. So he'd planned to cut out early, but after dancing with Lisa, he'd changed his mind. Damn, she felt good—soft in all the right places. And she smelled amazing, too. Her perfume reminded him of lemon blossoms.

Matt came to a stop and pointed to a shiny black Dodge Ram, the new registration sticker still taped to the passenger side of the windshield. "There's my truck."

The driver's door was open, the window shattered. On the seat, amidst shards of broken glass, sat a good-size rock.

"It would have been easy enough for you to check and see if that envelope was still there," Adam said. "Why didn't you?"

"Because I know how fussy you cops can be about disturbing a crime scene. But something else is *definitely* missing, which doesn't make a lot of sense."

"What's that?"

"My *food*. I hadn't eaten since the crack of dawn, so on my way here, I picked up something to tide me over at Bubba's Burger Barn. The bag was on the passenger seat, and now it's gone."

Adam furrowed his brow. "Someone took your leftovers?"

Matt scoffed. "Hell, it wasn't table scraps. It was a double bacon cheeseburger with large fries, and I didn't get the chance to take a single bite. I was going to eat it on the way over here, but as soon as I pulled out of the drive-through, my cell phone rang. And by the time the call ended, I'd already arrived at the party. So I decided to check out the fancy, hundred-dollar food first."

Adam scanned the area. The ground was still damp and a bit muddy from last night's rain, revealing small shoe prints—two sets, plus paw prints. All of which were fresh.

"Amateurs," Adam said. "Kids, most likely. Young ones. You mentioned the dog. It might be theirs."

"I'm pretty sure it was a stray. It had that scruffy, scrawny look. And it was tricolored—black, brown and what might be white if someone gave it a bath. I saw it when I was parking, and then again when I came back outside to eat my burger, which I figured was going to taste a heck of a lot better than those fancy tidbits they were putting out. That's when I saw that someone had broken into my truck."

"Did you notice anyone hanging around or hear anything?"

"No, but if they were anywhere nearby, they would have heard my reaction. I just bought that truck last week. So when I saw the broken glass, I swore loud enough to scare off the mutt. If there were kids anywhere around, they probably hightailed it out of here, too."

Adam reached beneath the seat, retrieved the yellow manila envelope stuffed with cash and handed it to Matt. "You might want to count it."

He fingered the thickness. "It feels like it's all here." Then he looked inside and counted it.

Apparently the young burglars had only wanted the food. Or else they'd been scared off before they could find anything of value.

Call it a hunch, or the memory of his own personal history, but something told Adam those kids were in some kind of trouble and that he'd better find them. And not just to put the fear of the law into them.

"Do you have insurance?" he asked.

"Yeah, but with a big deductible." Matt swore under his breath. "Why do you think the damn kids did this?"

"I suspect they were hungry."

Matt seemed to think on that for a couple of beats. "What are you going to do about it?"

"I'm going to look for them." And quickly. He wanted to return to the party before Lisa, the sexy intergalactic goddess, decided to leave.

While Matt remained near his truck, picking up the shards of glass and placing them in a burlap sack he'd found behind the driver's seat, Adam tracked the small footprints to a wooded area outside the grange hall and continued along the path they'd taken until he reached what appeared to be an abandoned, rusted-out paneled truck.

He didn't have his gun on him, but his gut told him

he wouldn't need it. His steps slowed as he approached the vehicle. When he got close enough, he peered through the grimy driver's-side window and spotted a young boy, a smaller girl and a scruffy mutt sitting in the cab sharing Matt's burger and fries. The kids didn't look much cleaner or better fed than the dirty dog.

As Adam opened the door, the mutt barked, and the children's eyes widened in apprehension. The dark-haired boy, who was about six or seven, slipped a bone-thin arm around his little blonde companion.

The moment Adam spotted her bruised cheek and her swollen, split lip, she commanded his full attention.

"Hey, guys." Adam offered his friendliest smile. "What's going on?"

Neither child uttered a word. The dog, its fur matted, merely cocked its head.

Adam scanned the interior of the dusty, beat-up vehicle. "This is a cool fort you guys have."

The kids remained silent, eyes leery. Something had them scared, and Adam doubted it was him.

"I know I'm not wearing a uniform," Adam said, "but I'm a police officer. And I'd like to help you."

The boy bit down on his bottom lip and studied Adam carefully, then he lifted his chin. "We ain't going home. And I'm not telling you where we live, either."

Kids often ran away from good homes, but given the overall undernourished appearance and defensive nature of these two, instinct told Adam that wasn't the case. And so did the girl's injury.

"I figure you two have a good reason for being out here."

When he was met with tight-lipped silence, he continued his questioning, attempting to be kind and gentle as he ferreted out what he already suspected. "Did someone at your house hurt you?"

"Yeah," the boy said indignantly. "He hurt my sister just because she peed her pants. It was an accident, and I cleaned it up. But he didn't care. He still spanked her. And he ain't even our dad."

Whether one believed in spanking or not, striking a child in the face was flat-out abuse. And doing so hard enough to leave a mark was criminal.

"Who is *he*?" Adam asked. "Your dad? Stepdad?"

"No, he's just a guy. The one who lived with us before our mama went away and didn't come back. But it's not like he takes care of us anyway."

Adam's gut clenched, and his thoughts took a personal turn as painful memories welled to the surface. He tamped them down the best he could, but his heart went out the poor kids, just as it always did when he came across other abused and neglected children. And he vowed to make sure that, when these two did go home, from now on, it was to a safe place, where a proper guardian would see that they had food to eat, clean clothes to wear and warm beds in which they could sleep.

"What's the guy's name?" Adam asked.

"Brady."

Adam nodded, making a mental note. "And what's your name?"

Again, the boy bit down on his lip, struggling to be strong. Holding on to his secret. Finally, he looked up and frowned. "If I tell you, are you going to promise to leave us alone and not take us back?"

"I *won't* take you back. But I'm not going to leave you alone, either. It's going to get cold—and it might rain again tonight. You'll also be hungry by morning."

Most law enforcement officers would turn the kids over to child protective services and then go about their way.

Sure, they might sympathize and regret the crappy environment those children had once lived in, but Adam wasn't like the others. Seeing kids who'd been beaten and mistreated hit a little too close to home.

He knew how it felt to be scared and sent to the county receiving home, where kids waited until social services placed them in foster care. Most of the parents were kind and good, but some weren't. So he hated the thought of turning in the brother and sister to the authorities and leaving them to the luck of the draw.

"My name is Adam," he told them, "although my friends sometimes call me Pancho."

The boy furrowed his brow. "Why do they call you that?"

"They were just messing with me, I guess. And the nickname stuck."

The kid seemed to chew on that for a minute, then said, "I'm Eddie. And this is my sister, Cassie. Are you really going to help us?"

"You bet I am." And this was one of those times he'd do it in his own way, which meant he'd have to pull a few strings.

At the sound of approaching footsteps, Adam turned to see Matt heading toward them.

"I'm glad you're here," Adam told his buddy. "I want you to meet my new friends, Eddie and Cassie."

Matt furrowed his brow, but didn't comment.

"I've got a few calls to make," Adam said, "but I need you to do me a favor. Would you find Jim and Donna Hoffman and bring them out here?"

"Sure. I'll do that, but what am I supposed to tell them?"

Adam was about to say that Eddie and Cassie needed a special place to stay tonight, but he suddenly had a light bulb moment. "I have a better idea. Why don't you bring out Santa and Mrs. Claus. They'll know just what to do. And I think the kids will feel a lot better about going home with them."

Matt nodded, then walked back to the Grange Hall.

Adam took a deep breath, then turned back to the kids.

"Do you really know Santa Claus?" Eddie asked.

"Yeah, I do."

Eddie chuffed. "He doesn't like me or Cassie. He never comes to our house."

Adam reached into the cab and placed a fatherly hand on Eddie's small, bony shoulder. "Actually, he really does like you. It's just that no one told him where you lived."

The kid looked skeptical. "How do you know that?"

"Because he didn't come to my house until I was practically grown up. And so one day, when I met him,

I asked him point blank why he'd forgotten me. And that's what he told me."

Eddie seemed to ponder that explanation.

"Do you live far from here?" Adam asked, hoping to get an idea where he could find Brady.

The boy stiffened. "You said you wouldn't take us back there."

"I won't. But I'd like to let Brady know it's against the law for him to hit people in the face, especially when they're smaller than he is."

"Maybe, if we would've run away sooner, and you found us before our mama left, she wouldn't have had to run away and hide from Brady, either."

Had the mother left her kids with the abuser and run away without them? It didn't seem likely, but Adam kept his thoughts to himself until he could investigate this case further.

And when he found Brady, they were going to have a little heart-to-heart, which would end up with Brady wearing cuffs and sitting in the back of a patrol car.

Adam sucked in a deep breath, filling his lungs with the crisp evening air. He wanted to tell them that life was going to get a lot better for them from now on, but he knew better than to make a promise he might not be able to keep. "I know of a perfect place for you two to hang out until something better comes along."

"What about our dog?" Eddie stroked the dirty critter's matted hair. "He doesn't have anyone to take care of him."

"Don't worry about that." Adam studied the scrawny, timid mutt. He'd have to call animal control, although it was after hours, and the stray would probably run off before anyone arrived. "I'll make sure he gets a bath, a bowl of food and a warm bed—just like you'll get."

Eddie's eyes, while cautious, betrayed hope. "You promise?"

"Cross my heart." Adam didn't know exactly how he was going to fulfill that promise, but he'd figure out a way. And once he knew those kids were safe, warm and fed, he'd return to the gala. If he was lucky, he'd be able to spend a little more time with Lisa, the woman he suspected would prove to be his "perfect" match.

Zorro never returned for his mask. In fact, after the cowboy took the Hoffmans outside, they left the party and didn't come back, either. Julie had no idea what had happened to them or where they'd gone on a Saturday night, but as she'd promised Jim, she drove out to Kidville on Monday morning.

She'd seen pictures on their website. The group home was set up like a small town in the Old West, complete with wooden sidewalks. Various buildings, such as a livery stable, a newspaper office and a hotel, appeared to be authentic in those photos, and she was looking forward to seeing it in person.

While online, she'd also done some research on the Hoffmans. From what she'd gathered, the couple had always dreamed of creating a place in the country where they could provide a safe, loving environment for abused and neglected city kids. After retiring from their county jobs in their mid-fifties, they set their plan in motion, a plan that was nearly two years in the making. Funding had been their biggest stumbling block—and apparently, at times, it still was. But thanks to the help of the community church, the Wexler Women's Club and the Brighton Valley Rotary, they remodeled the two-story ranch house, got it up to code, painted the barn and set up a playground. Then they added the Old West buildings.

Julie followed the county road about five miles out of town and turned into the drive. When she reached a black wrought iron gate, she used an intercom/phone system to request entrance.

The man who answered her call sounded like Jim Hoffman. "Come on in," he said. "The administration office is located in the Kidville Hotel."

Once the wrought iron gate swung open, granting her access to the property, she drove to a graveled lot and parked. She took her purse from the empty passenger seat, then opened the trunk and withdrew her guitar and a case filled with her musical bag of tricks—colorful scarves, kazoos, maracas, miniature tambourines and other rhythm instruments.

Then she locked the car and walked through an arched entryway made of adobe brick. A wooden overhead sign announced: Welcome to Kidville, Texas. Population 134.

Up ahead, she spotted a red schoolhouse. Behind it was a playground with swings, slides and a colorful climbing structure. To the right and left were grassy areas that provided a volleyball court on one side and a baseball field on the other. Kidville was even more appealing than she'd thought it would be. It was a unique setting, and one Julie hoped to be a part of one day soon.

She made her way to the administration office. Once she opened the door, she spotted Mr. Hoffman. The balding, heavyset man might not be dressed as Santa today, but when he greeted her with an easy smile, he still maintained a jolly demeanor.

"Thanks for coming, Julie." He paused. "It is Julie, isn't it?"

"Yes, that's right."

"I'm usually pretty good with names, but I'm afraid things got a little hectic on Saturday night."

Apparently so. The man and his wife had disappeared about the same time Zorro had, which prompted her to discreetly quiz him about it.

"I was surprised that you left so early," she said. "I'd planned to introduce myself to your wife, too."

"We had a little…" He glanced over his shoulder at a closed door, then lowered his voice. "One of our mentors who was attending the gala found a couple of runaways that night. And they were in desperate need of a safe place to live. So my wife and I brought them here. They were pretty frightened and uneasy, so we didn't want to leave them with our evening staff. So Donna and I stayed with them and helped them get settled."

Was Zorro the mentor who'd found the kids?

Julie was tempted to ask, but she thought better of getting too specific with her questions and hoped that the head of Kidville would provide her with more information on his own. "It sounds as if you, your wife and that mentor were at the right place and at the right time, Mr. Hoffman."

"Please, call me Jim. And you're right. Those kids had been through a lot. But Adam will get to the bottom of it."

"Adam?" she asked.

Jim nodded. "Adam Santiago. He's a police officer with Wexler PD. He found the children and realized they needed to be removed from their home."

Zorro had indicated he was in law enforcement, but hadn't the cowboy called him Pancho? From her college Spanish class, she'd learned that Pancho was a nickname for Francisco.

A bit confused, Julie said, "I'm glad to know those kids are here with you now. And that they're safe."

"So am I. In fact, my wife is talking to them now." Jim led the way through the reception area, which looked like a cozy living room filled with overstuffed sofas and chairs upholstered in faux leather. "Have a seat."

Julie placed her guitar case on the floor and, after sitting on the sofa, leaned the instrument against the arm rest.

Mr. Hoffman took a seat on one of the overstuffed chairs. He again glanced at the closed door, then lowered his voice. "The children seemed to connect with Adam on Saturday night. In fact, they didn't want him to leave. He stayed with them until nearly ten o'clock, then he promised them he'd be back this morning."

"Wasn't he able to come Sunday?" she asked. It was

what she would have promised them, had she been the one to find them.

"He wanted to investigate their prior living arrangement, and while he told *me* that he'd try to stop by then, Adam doesn't make promises he can't keep. At least, not to any of our children."

"I can appreciate that."

"Me, too. Adam was a foster kid himself, so he knows what many of our children have been through and how they feel. He's been mentoring some of the older boys for the past six months."

"How are the two new children doing now?" Julie asked. "Are they adjusting?"

"Cassie—she's the younger one—hasn't spoken a word since she arrived. And she won't let go of her brother's hand. Eddie's pretty protective of her, but he's a little skittish around adults."

"Those poor kids." Julie's heart went out to them, and she hadn't even met them yet.

The door squeaked open, and both Julie and Jim turned and watched a matronly woman walk out. She wore a conservative white blouse, black slacks and a pair of sensible walking shoes. A pair of small black barrettes held the sides of her salt-and-pepper hair in place.

Two children, a small boy with dark hair and a younger blonde girl who clung to his hand, trailed after her, followed by a tall, slender redhead in her late fifties.

She and Jim got to their feet, and he introduced Julie first to his wife Donna, the attractive redhead, then to Lyla Kincaid, the social worker assigned to the children's case.

They shook hands, and Julie said, "It's nice to meet you."

"Same here." Ms. Kincaid smiled, then turned to the children. "I'll see you in a few days. In the meantime, I'm glad you feel safe and comfortable here."

Jim walked the older woman to the door, while Donna introduced Julie to the children—six-year-old Eddie and his five-year-old sister, Cassie.

They looked thin and pale. Cassie bore a bruise on her forehead, as well as a split lip. No wonder Adam had rescued them. Whether he'd been the hottie dressed as Zorro or not, he'd turned out to be a real-life hero.

"Mr. Adam isn't here yet," Jim told the children. "But I'm sure he'll be here soon."

Donna placed one hand on the boy's shoulder and the other on his sister's. "Eddie and Cassie are nervous about going to meet their teacher this morning. So I thought it might be best if we waited for Mr. Adam to get here. They might feel better about going with him to the schoolhouse."

If Adam was the one who'd found them and rescued them from an abusive situation, they'd probably bonded.

"When is Mr. Adam coming?" Eddie asked. "I want to talk to him. To see if he did what he promised to do."

"He'll be here soon," Donna said. "And I'm sure he did exactly what he told you he'd do. He always keeps his word."

If Adam and Zorro were one and the same, as Julie

had begun to believe, then maybe she'd been wrong to assume he was a ladies' man and a charmer.

She wasn't sure what he'd promised the children—or why Eddie seemed so anxious to talk to him. But maybe, while they waited for him to arrive, she could help.

"If you'll come over here and sit with me," Julie told the children, as she took a seat on the sofa, "I have something I'd like to show you."

Neither child spoke, but they made their way to the sofa and sat beside her, watching intently as she unzipped her guitar case, withdrew the instrument and strummed a few chords.

She'd worn her hair long this morning, so she tucked the strands hanging forward behind her ears. Then she began to strum the chords of a silly song she hoped they'd find appealing.

As she played and sang, lulling the children the way she used to calm her daddy whenever he was stressed or anxious, she did her best to focus on the kids. Yet her eyes continued to drift toward the door, waiting for Adam's grand entrance. And to see if he was the gorgeous hunk who'd lured her onto the dance floor on Saturday night, then left her both charmed and hoping that he'd return—just as he'd promised.

Adam arrived at the Kidville gate about fifteen minutes later than he'd planned and used the code Jim had given him when he first began volunteering. After parking the Bronco, he headed for the hotel. He liked the Old West vibe of the place, although he preferred to hear the happy sounds of children at play. Apparently, school had already started.

Still, as he neared the admin office, he heard another sound—music. The guitar strums and a soft, melodic voice grew louder with each step he took.

As he let himself inside, he was stunned by the vision he saw, and his steps stalled. A twenty-something blonde wearing a long, colorful gypsy skirt and a soft green blouse sat on the overstuffed sofa, flanked by Eddie and Cassie. The kids were smiling as she sang a lively tune, her voice soft and melodic, her facial expression animated.

She seemed familiar, but then, Adam had an affinity for blondes.

He remained in the doorway, lulled by the sounds of the stringed instrument and the voice of an angel.

But it was Jim Hoffman's voice that drew him back to earth. "Adam, I'm glad you're here."

Oh. Yeah. He had a purpose, which didn't include being lured by a pretty musician.

"Am I late?" Adam asked.

"No, not really. But the kids have been waiting for you since breakfast. I told them you wouldn't let them down. That is, unless an emergency came along."

He continued to stand in the reception area, watching the kids. They seemed to be so caught up in the song that they didn't know he'd arrived. Neither did the singer.

Adam nodded his head toward the woman with the golden voice. "Who's that?"

"Julie Chapman. She's a new volunteer. She's also

a music therapist—and a good one, apparently. The kids are enthralled."

So was Adam. Back in the day, when he'd been in foster care and in trouble more times than not, one of his social workers had placed him in therapy, but he'd been resistant. He'd never warmed up to the shrink, who'd probably been an intern. Either way, he'd refused to play games like Parcheesi with him. And back then he damn sure wasn't going to let anyone into his head, so he'd clammed up until the rookie counselor finally threw in the towel.

But Adam hadn't realized therapy might consist of music—and a pretty blonde guitarist with an amazing voice.

"Julie's going to be a nice addition to our program," Jim said. "Don't you think?"

Adam nodded in agreement. He was certainly impressed by the way she'd enchanted the kids.

"Julie plays several instruments," Jim added, "including the piano. She majored in music while in college, and she's involved in her church choir."

Now, there was a game changer. Adam made a point of avoiding the good-girl type because he'd come to learn that they usually expected far more from him than a good time and a few laughs. But that didn't mean he couldn't watch them from afar. There was something about Julie he found appealing. In fact, she reminded him of Lisa, the sexy flight attendant he'd danced with at the gala. Funny how the two women, who couldn't possibly be more different from each other, struck him as similar.

The office telephone rang, and Jim excused himself. "I need to get that. Donna is in the back office. She's on hold with someone from tech support, so she's tied up at the moment."

As Jim crossed the room to his desk, Julie looked up and spotted Adam. Her lips parted, as if his arrival— or maybe his appearance—caught her by surprise. So much so, that she missed a couple of strums on the guitar and momentarily stopped singing. But she quickly recovered and turned her attention back to the children.

Adam didn't think anything of it. Women, even those who weren't his type, often found him attractive, which made his dating life easy. It also kept him busy. But from day one, he always made sure he and his dates were on the same page and that they realized he wasn't the kind of man who'd ever settle down.

When the catchy tune ended, Cassie reached out and touched Julie's guitar with her index finger, the first move Adam had seen her make without her brother's prompting. It might not seem like much to anyone else, but he saw it as a sign that the timid little girl wasn't nearly as frightened as she'd been on Saturday night when he and the Hoffmans had brought her here.

When he'd told the kids that he had to leave and that they'd be staying at Kidville, big ol' tears welled in her eyes, and her little lip quivered. Which is why he'd been eager to return this morning and let both kids know that he hadn't abandoned them. Hell, even the dog had gotten spooked and run off before the Hoffmans had showed up.

Adam waited a beat before crossing the room and

addressing the two siblings. "Hey, Eddie. Cassie. I'm back, just like I promised."

The boy practically jumped up from his seat, his lips parted, his eyes wide. "Cool. But what about your other promise? What happened to my dog? Did you find him?"

"Yes, I did." Adam glanced first at Jim, then back to Eddie. "She's a little skittish, but she's doing okay."

"She?" Eddie scrunched his brow and frowned. "Are you sure it's a *girl* dog?"

"Yep. I figured that out when I gave her a bath. That's not a problem, is it?"

Eddie shrugged a scrawny shoulder. "Only because I named her Spike. Now I have to think up something girly."

Adam glanced at Cassie, who didn't offer up a suggestion. In fact, she didn't utter a word.

"So where is she now?" Eddie asked.

A grin tugged at Adam's lips, and he slowly shook his head. "She's at my place temporarily." He'd actually be tempted to keep her, although he wasn't home much. "But don't worry. I'll find the perfect place for her. And who knows, maybe when you have a house with a yard, you can take her to live with you."

The little boy tensed, his smile faded and his eyes grew wide in near panic. "Are you going to take us back to Brady?"

"No way." Adam shook his head definitively. "You're much better off here. Don't you think?"

Eddie's expression softened and he nodded. Then

he glanced at his sister and back to Adam. "Cassie likes it here, too."

Adam studied the fair-haired girl who'd let her brother do all the talking on Saturday night. Something told him she still hadn't spoken. But he suspected she was coming around. At least, Julie and her music seemed to have gotten through to her.

And speaking of Julie, he'd better introduce himself. "I'm Adam Santiago. I volunteer here, too."

"It's…" She licked her glossed lips, pink and plump. "It's nice to meet you."

Before Adam could say anything else, Jim ended his phone call and joined them.

"Why don't we go for a walk with the kids?" Jim suggested. "We can take them to the schoolhouse and introduce them to their teacher."

"Can I go, too?" Julie asked.

"By all means," Jim said. "I'm sure the kids will like that."

Julie turned to the children. "I saw the school and the playground when I first got here, and it looks like you'll have a lot of fun during recess. I'd love to see the inside of the classroom."

Eddie shot a look at Jim, then at Adam, and back to Jim again. "Okay, but can Cassie come with me—and *stay* with me? She doesn't like to be alone."

"You bet," Jim said. "We only have a single classroom and one teacher right now, although we're planning to expand in the future. So our school is a little different from the one you're used to."

"I had a class and a teacher once," Eddie said, "but it was a long time ago. And Cassie never did."

That wasn't surprising. From what Adam had gathered during his investigation of Brady Thatcher, the guy hadn't played any kind of paternal role with the kids. Hell, he hadn't even noticed they were gone until Adam showed up at his door and told him.

It was a real shame, too. If the kids had gone to school, a teacher might have picked up on their abuse and neglect sooner.

The telephone rang again, and Jim straightened. "Oh, for Pete's sake. I'm never going to get these kids to school."

"Go ahead and take that call," Adam said. "I'll walk with them to their classroom and introduce them to their teacher."

Julie, who'd just put her guitar into its case, looked up and smiled. "I'm ready to go with you."

As they exited the admin office and walked along the wooden sidewalk toward the school, a light breeze kicked up, stirring the air around them, as well as a few strands of Julie's long blond hair and a whiff of her scent—something citrusy.

Adam stole another peek at her, but the quick glance turned into a steady gaze. He noted her pretty profile. Long, thick lashes. A light dusting of freckles across a slightly turned up nose. Plump, kissable lips. Once again, he caught her scent and considered her similarity to Lisa, the flight attendant he'd danced with at the gala. Apparently their perfume was the latest fashion craze.

He was so caught up with his assessment of Julie that he damn near tripped when they stepped off the wooden boardwalk. He'd better shake off his thoughts and interest before she caught him studying her. Or worse, before he did a face-plant in the dirt.

"I used to love school," Julie told Eddie and Cassie. "I didn't have any brothers or sisters, so being on the playground at recess gave me a chance to have a lot of fun with the other kids."

An only child, huh? The apple of her daddy's eye, no doubt. And her mama's pride and joy. Adam had known girls like her, and they'd all steered clear of guys like him, which was just as well. He preferred simple, unencumbered relationships that lasted until one or the other got bored and moved on to someone else.

When they reached the red schoolhouse, he slowed to a stop. "This is it."

He figured the teacher was expecting the kids, so he opened the door, and they stepped inside the large room that smelled like pencil shavings, crayons and paste.

The teacher, Mrs. Wright, a blonde in her mid-thirties, was walking among the children and passing out math worksheets, none of which seemed to be the same level.

When Jesse Cosgrove, the kid Adam had been mentoring, glanced at the doorway, he brightened and waved. "Hey! Mr. Adam, it's not Wednesday."

Adam placed his index finger on his lips, shushing him, then he lifted it in the air and made a circular motion, indicating that the boy should turn around and focus on his work. He followed the silent chastisement with a wink, letting the kid know they'd talk later.

Jesse seemed to understand because he spun in his seat and faced the front of the class. As he studied the math worksheet on his desk, he scrunched his brow, stuck his pencil in his mouth and bit down on what was left of his eraser. Jesse was the oldest boy at Kidville, but he lagged a couple of years behind academically.

"This is what they call a combination class," Adam told Julie and the kids, repeating what Jim had told him during his first tour of the place. "At this time, they're only licensed to take children up to the third grade. And from what I've heard, Cassie is going to be the only kindergartener."

Mrs. Wright passed out one last worksheet, then strode to the doorway, stooped and greeted Eddie and Cassie by name. "We were excited to hear we'd have two new friends in class. And we've been waiting to meet you. As soon as the other children finish their math, it'll be time for morning snack and recess."

Both Eddie and Cassie seemed nervous, but Mrs. Wright was a champ when it came to putting children at ease. So it wouldn't take long for her to make the two siblings feel welcome. Once she took them to their desks, Adam and Julie left their little charges and headed back the admin office.

Again, Adam caught a hint of her lemon-blossom fragrance.

"Can I ask what perfume you're wearing?" he asked.

Julie's steps slowed, and her lips parted. "Excuse me?"

"Your perfume. It's so familiar to me."

"Thank you. It's my shampoo, actually." She picked up her pace, which compelled him to quicken his steps, too.

"Whatever it is," he said, "It's nice. It reminds me of…someone I know." Lisa. His erstwhile dance partner from the gala. The two women had lots of things in common. Their hair color, their petite stature. Of course, Lisa had been dressed in that skimpy space avenger outfit, and Julie wore a long-sleeve blouse and a skirt that was nearly floor length. She didn't seem to be the kind of woman who'd be comfortable showing that much skin.

For a moment, he wondered if they might be the same woman, then he quickly discarded the notion. He'd been told Lisa was fun-loving. A risk-taker, like he was.

Adam might follow the rules these days, but he still had a rebellious side that didn't mix well with good girls who sang in the choir and who had very specific ideas about what they wanted in life.

He stole another glance at Julie. She'd certainly dressed the part this morning, but he couldn't help envisioning her in that sexy costume. A grin tugged at his lips. What was lurking under the surface?

It might be fun to find out, but Adam decided he'd better rein in his imagination. He didn't date good girls—at least not intentionally. And the smart ones who'd managed to trick him into believing they had a wild side knew better than to go out with him more than once.

Chapter Three

Apparently, Julie's efforts to wear a mask and keep a low profile at the Autumn Gala had worked even better than she'd hoped. Adam had no idea that he'd seen her on Saturday night or that they'd danced together. But she'd seen *his* face clearly enough.

Just minutes ago, when she'd spotted him in the Kidville office, her heart had taken a flying leap, making it difficult to stay on track, to remember the words of the silly song she'd been singing to the kids. Fortunately, she'd recovered quickly. And now here she was, walking along with one of Wexler PD's finest. And no doubt one of their hottest.

Too bad he was off-limits. She made a point of avoiding men who had high-stress, dangerous jobs. She'd seen firsthand the effect that could have on a man. And the experience had been so painful that she'd broken up with her college boyfriend when he told her he planned to join the military.

Still, she found herself attracted to Adam. And intrigued by him.

"Jim was telling me that you were the one who found the kids," Julie said.

"They'd broken into my buddy's truck and stolen a bag of food he'd left on the seat. But I can't blame them. Brady Thatcher, the guy who was supposed to be looking out for them, was a real loser. He didn't give a damn about them, and the poor kids were starving."

"They're pretty thin," Julie said. "I'm no pediatrician, but they appear to be malnourished."

"I'm sure you're right. Who knows when they last saw a doctor or dentist?"

"Did you go to their house?"

Adam nodded, as they walked back to the admin office. "Once Eddie opened up and gave me enough details to find the house, which was just as neglected as the kids, I arrested Brady for child abuse, as well as a parole violation for possession of a controlled substance."

"How long will he be in jail?"

"Quite a while. He had several convictions for assault, as well as a drunk and disorderly."

"I take it that means he'll have to relinquish custody."

"Turns out that he never had it in the first place. When their mom disappeared, the kids ended up with him."

"That's too bad."

"It sure is."

As they walked slowly, Julie's shoulder brushed against Adam's, warming her and setting off a tingly sensation. Yet he continued as if he hadn't felt anything at all.

She stole a glance at him, wishing she didn't find him so attractive. And so honorable. Clearly, he still didn't recognize her because she'd worn a mask on Saturday night, but he'd removed his before leaving the gala.

A smile tickled her lips. Even if he hadn't revealed his face, she had a feeling she would have recognized him anyway—those expressive brown eyes, that dazzling smile. He also had a distinctive voice laced with a slight accent, making it smooth, masculine and alluring.

On top of that, there was something about the way he walked, the way he carried himself. He had a swagger that would be difficult for another man to imitate. And one a woman couldn't ignore.

As they approached the office, Adam shared some of what Eddie had told him on Saturday night. "He said his mom was nice when she wasn't drinking, but she drank a lot after Brady moved in with them. I did a background check before going to the house and learned he had a mean streak, even when he was sober. And he'd had a tendency to strike anyone who crossed him."

"Did Eddie say what happened to his mom?"

"One day, probably while school was out for the

summer, Eddie heard them fighting in the bedroom, and when they came out, his mom had a bloody nose. She claimed that she fell while getting out of the bathtub. Then she told him to watch Cassie while she and Brady went out for a little while."

"He's way too young to be babysitting now, let alone a year ago."

"I know. But apparently, he's been looking after Cassie for a long time. Anyway, Brady came back alone that night. He told Eddie that his mom was going to be a famous movie star. Supposedly she met a Hollywood big shot at the Rusty Wagon."

"What's that?" Julie asked.

"It's a seedy bar where they used to hang out. According to what Brady told Eddie, the guy thought his mom was pretty and took her to California."

It sounded bogus to Julie. "Do you believe any of that story?"

"Hell no." Adam scoffed. "It's my job to sniff out lies, and that one stunk to high heaven."

"I can be a Pollyanna at times," Julie admitted, "but I have to agree with you. Hollywood producers don't hang out in seedy Texas bars."

"Exactly." Adam slowed his already casual pace, then he stopped altogether in front of the Kidville newspaper office. "On Saturday night, when I told the kids I had to go home and was leaving them with the Hoffmans, they both begged me to stay."

"That's not surprising. You're their hero, the man who saved them."

Adam shrugged off the praise. "I did what any other

law enforcement officer would've done. But their teary eyes and quivering lips damn near turned me inside out."

"It would have done the same to me."

"Yeah, well, I don't usually allow myself to get sucked into emotional quagmires like that, but for some reason, Eddie and Cassie got to me. And come hell or high water, I'm going to find out what actually happened to their mother."

Julie didn't mean to pepper him with so many questions, but there was a lot she wanted to know. She'd taken an interest in the kids this morning, when her songs had drawn shy smiles.

"Did you tell them you were going to look for their mom?" she asked.

"Yes, and I filed a missing person report. But I hate to give the kids any false hope. I don't have a good feeling about her disappearance."

"What about their father?" she asked, feeling a bit like a Kidville star reporter. "Where is he?"

"Eddie told me he died when Cassie was a tiny baby."

"That's so sad. Do they have grandparents or another relative?"

"Looking for family members is on my to-do list. If there's someone out there who's willing to take them, they won't have to remain wards of the state." Adam leaned against the wooden porch railing and blew out a sigh. "I could have called protective services that night, but I knew Kidville would be a better place for them than the receiving home."

"I wondered why you left so quickly."

At that, Adam zeroed in on her, his brow slightly furrowed. "Were you at the gala?"

He'd just given her the perfect opportunity to set him straight. "I work for the caterer and was serving that night."

His gaze roamed over her. "Well, I'll be damned. You were the blonde in that space avenger costume. I noticed the similarities, but I'd been told that a woman named Lisa would be there. And I'd assumed you were her. I'm sorry. I didn't recognize you without your... uh...costume."

Julie looked down at her shoes—a pair of flats— then back at Adam. "I guess you didn't recognize Lisa, either."

At that, he laughed. "You've got that right. I'd never met her before. I'd only been given a description of her."

"So it was going to be a blind date?"

"I guess you could say that. I've never had any use or need for a matchmaker, but Stan..." He paused, and his expression sobered for a beat. "A mutual friend of ours, had been trying to set us up for a while. And I figured I'd bypass the awkwardness and introduce myself."

They stood there for a moment. No doubt, trying to make sense of it all. Had Julie and Adam been destined to meet? Or was it just a weird coincidence?

"You didn't correct my mistake that night," he said. "Why?"

A slow smile stretched across her lips. "Because I

love music and thought it might be fun to dance one time before I had to serve appetizers. And just for the record, I would have set you straight, but you were called away before I got the chance."

"Sorry about that. I didn't mean to leave you stranded on the dance floor. That's not my style."

Julie didn't think it was.

"But it was fun while it lasted," he added.

Was it? She'd certainly enjoyed what little time they'd spent together.

"I owe you another dance," he said.

"No, you don't. I wasn't there to play around. I should have been working. And just so you know, being lazy isn't *my* style." With that, she stepped off the boardwalk and crossed the dusty street toward the hotel. Adam followed suit, but they remained silent. Lost in their thoughts, she supposed.

"So you're a music therapist," Adam finally said, when they reached the door. "That's an interesting occupation."

"Music has a powerful effect on people, on their mood, on their physical rehabilitation. And it provides an outlet for the expression of feelings. I've done two internships, one at a nursing home and another with autistic children, so I've seen firsthand how it works." She didn't tell him that she'd first discovered the calming effects of music on her father, who'd suffered from PTSD.

"Did you come from a musical family?" he asked.

"My mom used to be in a country-western band, but she quit when she got pregnant with me. She sang to me all the time, and when she noticed my interest and talent, she gave me piano lessons at home. And when I was in high school, I taught myself how to play the guitar."

"That's pretty cool." He lobbed her a smile that caressed her ego. "So now you're able to use what you learned and perform for kids."

"Actually, I've been performing for a while." Julie tucked a strand of hair behind her ear. "Whenever my dad was deployed, especially during the holidays, my mom and I would visit several convalescent hospitals and a veterans' home."

They continued to stand outside the hotel, assessing each other, it seemed. Or reassessing first impressions, she supposed. Adam wasn't just nice to look at—he was easy to talk to.

"You know," he said, "the Wexler Chamber of Commerce is hosting a dance next Saturday night. Why don't you go with me? I never stay very long at those kinds of events, but I can take you out on the dance floor once or twice."

"Are you asking me out?"

"If you're going to say yes, then that's exactly what I'm doing. But if you're going to say no, then I'm only trying to repay a debt."

Julie really should decline, but the moment their gazes locked, her heart fluttered, releasing a blood-stirring attraction she couldn't resist.

"All right," she said. "I'll go with you. Is the dance formal or casual? How should I dress?"

A boyish grin stretched across his face, and he gave

her a playful wink. "I don't suppose you'd agree to wear that intergalactic costume again."

She rolled her eyes at the absurdity. "Absolutely not." Yet the flirtatious suggestion complimented her in an unexpected way, and she couldn't help softening her response with a smile. "That skimpy thing is *so* not me."

"I was afraid you'd say that."

Had Julie known him better, she might have given him a playful punch to the arm. Instead, she shook her head, reached for the doorknob and entered the Kidville office.

As Adam followed her inside, so did a sense of apprehension about their upcoming date. Had she made a mistake by agreeing to it?

Adam wasn't a military veteran haunted by brutal wartime memories, but he could still be considered a civilian soldier who faced battles on the city streets. And while both types were considered heroes, she'd done her share of time dealing with the effects of a man tormented by PTSD.

Besides, she'd bet the farm that the handsome cop was a flirt and a ladies' man, another reason to avoid getting in too deep.

Common sense urged her to backpedal, to tell Adam that she'd just remembered something else she'd previously scheduled for Saturday night. To tell him that this time, she was the one offering a rain check—and one she'd find a way not to honor. But as she glanced over her shoulder at him and spotted the glimmer in those gorgeous brown eyes, she realized she wouldn't do that. The truth of the matter was, each time she stole a glance his way or caught a whiff of his woodsy scent, she was reminded of her brief encounter with Zorro. And she was swept away by the memory of his strength as he reached for her hand and guided her to the dance floor.

She could still recall the warmth of his body as she rested her cheek on his shoulder, the spike in her pulse rate and tingly sparks of excitement as they swayed to the heart-thumping beat, as if it had taken place just moments ago.

So how could she pass up the opportunity to experience that one more time?

On Wednesday afternoon, Adam drove out to Kidville to mentor Jesse Cosgrove, the ten-year-old boy who'd been acting out and giving the Hoffmans and his teacher a hard time.

Jesse's younger brother lived in a good foster home, one in which he seemed to be happy and thriving. The parents were some of the best Adam had ever seen, but while they were willing to take one more kid, they were reluctant to accept a known troublemaker.

After parking, Adam headed to the playground, where all the kids were at this time of day. In addition to Jesse, he was eager to check on Eddie and Cassie and see if they were settling in. Before he could make a full scan of the play areas, he spotted Julie pushing Cassie in a swing.

He'd been looking for the little girl, but it was Julie he zeroed in on. She was wearing a pair of black jeans and a ruffled white blouse. She'd pulled her hair back in a ponytail, which made her look especially wholesome today.

In spite of the fact that she wasn't his type—a realization his libido hadn't accepted yet—he approached her and flashed a smile. "I see that you have other talents besides singing and playing guitar."

"That's right," she said, a pretty smile spreading across her face, emerald-green eyes bright. "I'm also a swinging expert and part-time coach."

Adam scanned the sandbox, as well as the surrounding lawn area, and noticed Julie was the only adult outside. Usually there were two—Karen Wright, the teacher, and one of the Hoffmans.

"Are you a playground monitor, too?" Adam asked Julie.

"I am today." She continued to teach Cassie the fine art of pumping her feet to propel the swing by her own efforts. "That's it, sweetie. You've got it!"

It pleased him to see Cassie playing and not clutching her brother for a change, but he'd rather see her laughing and making friends her age.

As Julie took a couple of steps away from the little girl and moved closer to Adam, he said, "I take it you're volunteering here on Mondays *and* Wednesdays."

"For the time being." She lifted her hand, blocking the afternoon sunlight from her eyes. "In fact, when I'm not working for Silver Spoon Catering, I plan to spend most of my free time here."

"So besides being a music therapist, you're Jackie of all trades."

She scrunched her brow, tilted her head slightly and gave him a funny look that he found especially cute.

"That was supposed to be a joke," he said, "but I guess it was pretty lame. People usually think I'm pretty funny, but I'll admit some of my quips are better than others."

At that, Julie laughed, a lyrical sound that not only seemed fitting for a musician, but one he found alluring.

"You know," she said, a smile dimpling her cheeks, "I had you pegged as a charmer."

"I try to be. But I'll let you in on a secret. It doesn't work every time."

She laughed again, and he was determined to offer her his better quips, just to touch her funny bone.

But Adam wasn't here to flirt with the music therapist, so he searched the playground, where he spotted Eddie at the handball court. He'd also yet to find Jesse, who was probably inside the climbing structure where he couldn't be seen.

Jesse would eventually turn up, since he looked forward to their Wednesday afternoons, so Adam shrugged it off.

Still, it was odd that Julie was the only one on playground duty this afternoon, although the adult to child ratio was within state regulations.

"Looks like the teacher and administrators ditched you," he said. "Where is everyone?"

"Jim went into town for supplies, and Donna is working in the office. I'm just filling in while Karen is in the classroom supervising two boys who lost recess privileges for fighting during social studies."

"Don't tell me," Adam said. "One of them is Jesse Cosgrove."

"Yes," Julie said as she closed the gap between them. "How did you know?"

"Jesse's the one I've been mentoring. He's not a bad kid, but he's got a big chip on his shoulder and has been a general pain in the butt more times than not. Karen and Jim told me that he was doing better, so I've been cautiously optimistic that my time spent with him has been helpful. But maybe I need to rethink that."

Julie blessed him with a pretty smile and a playful wink. "Two steps forward, one step back."

"That's about the size of it. But Jesse has a good heart. And he always feels badly after he blows it. He just needs some guidance."

A soft afternoon breeze picked up, blowing a strand of Julie's blond hair that escaped her ponytail across her face. She brushed it away with her fingertips, her nails unpolished but neatly manicured.

As usual, he found her pretty—and appealing. He also found her sexy, when he really shouldn't.

Before he could come up with something nice yet generic to say, Eddie left his handball game and trotted up to the swing set, bypassing his younger sister. "Hey! Mr. Adam. How's my dog? Did you find him… I mean, *her*, a home yet?"

"Not yet." You'd never know that the boy only met the stray last Saturday night. But he supposed they'd both needed a friend. "Don't worry, Eddie. I'm work-ing on it."

In all honesty, Adam hadn't done a damn thing to find it a home. The timid little critter needed to spend some time with someone affiliated with a dog rescue organization before being sent off to live with a regu-lar family.

"Is it going to be hard to find a good place for her?" the boy asked. "I mean, she's a cool dog."

"Yeah, you're right. She's too skinny, though. So I thought I'd better fatten her up some. But don't worry. She's doing fine. You should have seen her on Sunday morning, after I chased her down, took her home and gave her a good bath. I'll bet you wouldn't recognize her now. That beige fur is snow white."

Eddie brightened. "Will you tell her I miss her and wish she could live at Kidville with us?"

"Sure. I'll tell her. In the meantime, until you get a house with a yard or I find a good home for her, she can stay with me." Besides, Adam wasn't in any big hurry to ditch the dog. She was a sweet little thing, but very timid. There was no way she was ready to join a fam-ily with a couple of active kids who'd probably scare the liver out of her.

Hell, even though he'd spoken softly to her and moved slowly, it had taken almost a day for him to en-courage her to come out from behind the chair she'd hid behind. She was coming out into the open a little more, even though her tail seemed permanently tucked behind her rear legs.

She also seemed to be warming up to him, which

was good. It was kind of nice to come home to a room-mate again, even if this one had four legs and a wet nose.

"I sure wish I could see her," Eddie said wistfully.

"Maybe," Adam said, "after she gets more comfortable and doesn't frighten so easily, I can bring her to visit you here."

"That would be awesome." Eddie smiled, revealing a gap in his front teeth, then turned and hurried back to the handball court, leaving Adam and Julie alone.

"I didn't want to overstep," Julie said, "but if the dog is so timid, she might find Kidville to be a little overwhelming. But I'm sure Jim and Sandra would let you take Eddie to your house."

Yeah, Adam figured the same thing. "I'd rather not invite him over yet. I'm still working with Jesse, and I'd like him to think our time together is special. He might even get jealous of Eddie, and who knows what that might lead to." He'd just have to wait and see how things played out after the teacher reprimanded Jesse for fighting. Those scoldings, while fair and needed, didn't always go over well.

Adam was about to change the subject when he caught Julie gazing at him. The breeze kicked up again, unleashing that loose strand of hair and stirring up a whiff of her lemon-blossom scent. His thoughts drifted to the dance they'd shared at the gala—as well as the one coming up on Saturday night.

"Would you like to get a bite to eat before we go to the dance sponsored by the Chamber of Commerce?" he asked.

She bit down on her bottom lip, nibbling at a coat of pink gloss. "I guess so. What did you have in mind?"

"Nothing fancy." But as he studied the pretty woman who had a girl-next-door vibe, he wondered if fancy might be a better option after all. She looked damn good to him now, but dressed to the nines in a sexy red cocktail dress and heels...

"I really hadn't given a restaurant any thought," he lied. "We could get pizza. Or burgers. There's also that new steak place in town. I've wanted to try it, but haven't had a chance to do so yet."

"I'm up for whatever you decide. Just let me know what I should wear."

"I'll need your phone number," he said.

She whipped her iPhone out of her pocket. "Give me your cell number and I'll call you. Then you'll have it."

He provided her with the number, then added. "I'll give you the one for the house, too."

"You still have a landline?"

"Yep. And it's even got an answering machine. My former roommate was an older guy, and he left it. And I've never taken the time to get a new setup."

Her head tilted slightly to the side, and skepticism filled her eyes. "Seriously?"

"Absolutely." But there was no way he'd ever get rid of it. "I'll tell you what. Call my house and let it roll over to the recording."

Adam provided the number, then watched her dial.

Moments later, after three rings, the answering machine would kick on. Adam didn't have to overhear

Stan's outgoing message. He'd memorized it a long time ago.

You've reached Stan and Adam. We can't get to the phone right now, but if you leave a message, one of us will get back to you when we can. Just keep in mind, with our busy schedules, it could be a couple of days.

Julie left her number, then she disconnected the call.

"Who's Stan?" she asked. "Your roommate?"

"He was."

"Did he move out?"

He hesitated. "Not exactly. He passed away about six weeks ago."

Her expression morphed into one of sympathy. "I'm sorry, Adam."

"Yeah, me, too. That's one reason I keep that old telephone and the answering machine. Right before he died, Stan called home and left me a message. And every now and then, I like to listen to his voice."

"He must have been a good friend."

"The best. He was a real stand-up guy." The kind a troubled kid had tried his best to emulate. The kind a grown man would always grieve.

"How'd it happen?" Julie asked.

Emotion wadded in his throat, and he cleared his voice in an attempt to dislodge it and shake it off. "A car accident. Drunk driver."

When he glanced at Julie, her eyes seemed a little watery. Before the emotion he'd learned to keep at bay returned, choking him, he said, "Besides, there's nothing wrong with being a little out of date. I'd think you'd appreciate my home telephone system. You strike me as the old-fashioned type."

"I guess you could say that."

He also suspected she was the quiet type, more prone to mellow evenings at home than wild parties.

As much as he liked gazing into her eyes, studying her profile when she wasn't looking and talking to her, he realized he'd probably made a huge mistake. Opposites might attract, but they often bumped heads in the long run.

And something told him he and Julie were on a collision course, because he had a feeling she would expect far more from him than he was willing to give.

Chapter Four

By Saturday afternoon, Adam had yet to call and tell Julie where they would be going for dinner. But that was okay. She'd already showered and shampooed her hair. All she had to do was snatch one of the two outfits she'd placed on top of her bed and slip it on.

She'd set out a classic little black dress and heels, which she would wear if he'd been able to get reservations at that new steakhouse. If he opted for pizza or burgers, she'd decided on a brightly colored, mid-calf length dress, a shoulder wrap to keep her warm and a new pair of flats.

She glanced out the window and spotted the setting sun, the waning light casting shadows in her room. Then she looked at the clock on the bureau, the minute hand marching toward the dinner hour.

I'll give you a call on Saturday to make plans, he'd told her.

While she waited, she'd better find something else to do, other than standing alone in her bedroom, stressing over which outfit to wear. She turned away from the bed, just as her cell phone rang. At the long-awaited sound, her pulse rate shot through the roof, and she nearly jumped out of her skin. She fumbled for the phone, and when she finally got a hold of it and spotted Adam's name on the display, her heart slammed against her chest. It took a moment to contain her excitement as she accepted the incoming call.

Get a grip, girl. She sucked in a fortifying breath, then slowly let it out before answering. But her breathy "Hello" came out a lot brighter than she'd wanted it to.

"Hey, Julie," Adam said. "I'm sorry to do this to you at the last minute, but I was assigned a big case earlier today, and I have to work late. So I can't go out tonight. Can we reschedule?"

Disappointment swelled in her throat, and it took a moment to tamp it down before she could risk a response.

"No problem," she said. "I understand. Things happen."

And often for a good reason. Had Fate stepped in to stop her from making a mistake by going out with a man who wasn't right for her?

"They sure do," Adam said. "Things like this seem to happen to me more often than not. My job often requires me to work overtime, and then my personal plans change."

Wasn't that another reason she couldn't pin her heart on him?

"I'll make it up to you," he added.

"That's okay. It's probably for the best anyway." Once the words rolled off her tongue, she realized they came out a little snappish and more truthful than she'd intended, so she softened them with a white lie. "I have quite a few things I really need to do tonight. In fact, I'd even thought about calling you and canceling. But you beat me to it."

She glanced at the outfits lying on her bed. The only thing she really had pending was hanging them back in her closet.

"I'll see you at Kidville," he said.

"You probably will." She'd actually been spending a lot of time there this past week, which gave her something to do while waiting for a job offer. Besides, she was trying to secure a position at Kidville, which seemed like a perfect fit for her. She liked the kids and the people who worked there. "I'll talk to you later, then. Maybe on Wednesday."

"Actually, I'll be there Monday. Like I said, my plans tend to change more often than not. And since I'm working this weekend, they gave me that day off. So I plan to take Jesse out for a pizza. And while I'm at it, he and I are going to have a little man-to-boy chat about fighting."

"Good idea," Julie said. "I'll see you then."

But she already knew how she'd respond if he tried to reschedule with her. *I'm sorry, Adam. I already have plans.* Imaginary ones, of course. But she'd come up with something believable.

In the meantime, she'd chalk up today as a lesson learned. She had no business going out with Adam in the first place. Any woman who dated him would soon learn that she'd always come in second place to his job. And that was just one more red flag, one more good reason to avoid him the best she could. Besides, weren't police officers prone to divorce? Maybe not all of them, but she'd read something somewhere. And she was determined to have a peaceful home, unlike the one she'd lived in with her father.

After ending the call, Julie hung her black dress back in the closet. As disappointment swirled inside her like bathwater circling the drain, she did her best to shake it off.

She told herself she'd actually dodged a bullet tonight. No matter how charming and handsome Adam might be, he was definitely the wrong guy for her. And she'd better not forget that.

Yet as she reached for the yellow dress, her resolve wavered, leaving her unsure about anything—especially her feelings and her assessment of Adam Santiago.

For the first time Adam could remember, canceling a date at the last minute left him feeling guilty. But then again, before today, he'd never had a phony reason for doing so. But the closer it got to the dinner hour on Saturday night, the more he regretted asking Julie out in the first place.

Not that he wasn't attracted to her. She seemed to grow prettier and more appealing each time he saw her. But she wasn't his type. He liked the risk-takers and fun-lovers who didn't expect anything long-term. And when he took Jesse back to Kidville on Wednesday evening, Jim Hoffman had pretty much confirmed his fears.

I noticed you eyeing Julie, Jim had said. *And I don't blame you. She's a keeper—the kind of woman a man takes home to meet his mom.*

Adam didn't have a mom. Not anymore. But he knew what Jim meant. Julie was a white-picket-fence type—and marriage wasn't in the cards for him.

So even if they'd gone out tonight and had a good time—and he didn't doubt they would have—he knew that, in the long run, one way or another, he'd end up disappointing her. So he figured that by pulling the I-have-to-work-overtime card he would save them both a lot of grief.

After hanging up, he tried to convince himself that he'd done the right thing, the noble thing. But he couldn't quite buy that. And now he felt more unsettled about the decision than he'd expected.

As if sensing Adam's conflicting thoughts, his temporary roommate let out a little whine.

Adam shot a glance at the tricolored stray who sat next to the brown leather recliner, studying him with timid eyes.

At least she wasn't hiding behind the chair. So he eased toward her, dropped to his knees and held out his hand for her to sniff. "Hey, doggie."

He waited as the seconds ticked by, wondering if she'd come to him this time. When she didn't, he made silly kissy sounds. When that didn't work, he went into the kitchen and pulled out a box of treats.

"Hey, girl. How 'bout a dog biscuit?"

To his mild surprise, she began to inch toward him, one scooch at a time, her tail thumping the floor.

You'd think that after he'd rescued her, given her a bath and flea dip, provided her with food and a warm place to park her furry butt, he wouldn't have to bribe her. She really should have figured out he was trustworthy a lot sooner than this.

"See?" he said. "I'm not going to hurt you."

She sniffed at his hand, then gave it a shy, tentative lick, the first sign of the progress they'd made. He rewarded her with the biscuit, which she wolfed down with gusto.

"You don't know this, but I'd planned to take you to the animal shelter right after I found you. Someone might have taken you home, and then I could've told Eddie you were doing great. But I didn't have the heart to do it."

He'd thought long and hard about it, though. If she had a microchip, the animal control officer might have been able to find her rightful owner. But when he'd studied the scrawny, neglected little critter, unexpected sympathy sucker-punched him.

Funny how that could happen. He'd even gone shopping at a pet store last Sunday afternoon and picked up a few toys, which she didn't play with, and a padded bed, which she only sniffed. Not that he planned to keep her. He'd send her things with her when he found her a new home.

Oh, yeah? he asked himself. *What about the doggie door you installed?*

What about it? he countered. *She has to be able to let herself outside when I'm not home.*

Adam scratched behind the dog's ear, letting her know he'd do right by her.

But who was he kidding? The dog deserved way more than he could give her. She needed a home with a family, although there was no way she'd be able to hold her own with any wild-ass kids who didn't know how to be patient or gentle.

No, he'd decided. Before she could possibly be adopted by a family, she'd need someone experienced at rescuing abused dogs to work with her until she was ready to transition to a real home.

It wouldn't be right for him to even think about keeping her. He'd have to let her go.

Kind of like he'd just done with Julie. He'd let her down gently, which would allow her to find the right guy, one who could give her everything she deserved.

Adam gave the dog one final stroke, then got to his feet, moving slowly so she didn't shy away—or dash back behind the recliner.

She didn't, which was a relief. But he still felt at a loss.

If Stan were still alive, Adam would have talked things over with him. He glanced at the old-style telephone and the answering machine that sat next to it. If he couldn't talk to Stan, he could listen to his voice and maybe he'd be able to imagine what his wise mentor might have said.

So he crossed the room, ignoring the black desk phone and going right to the answering machine. Then he pushed the play button to hear the message he'd saved.

"Hey, Adam. I won't be home tonight. I'm going to take Darlene on the town. That gal might be the one woman in the world who can change this ol' bachelor's mind about commitments.

"Yeah, yeah. You think I'm going soft. Believe it or not, I went the first fifty years of my life without getting roped into marriage, but then I met Darlene, and I actually like the idea of spending the rest of my life with her. Maybe it's time for you to find your Darlene, too."

Little had Stan known his last words to Adam had been prophetic. He actually had spent the rest of his life with Darlene. After dinner that night, while they were on their way to her house, a drunk driver ran a red light and broadsided their car, killing them both on impact.

Adam still grieved for his friend and mentor, and while listening to his voice was always bittersweet, it also had a way of centering him. But it hadn't worked out that way today. Instead, Stan's words had another impact. They set off a sense of loneliness and a longing for something elusive.

Hell, even if Adam wanted to settle down with one special lady, like Stan had hoped to do with Darlene, he didn't see himself falling in love with anyone. Even if he wanted to, he'd never be able to pull it off. He'd built up too many walls over the years, too many barriers—like the one that had made him cancel a date at the last minute.

He shot a glance at the dog, who'd remained in the same spot near the recliner, her head slightly bent in submission, leery eyes gazing at him as if she could read his mind.

"That's right," he told her. "How can I give a woman what she needs, when I can only provide you with the basics, like food, water and shelter? And you need more than that. You deserve to live with someone who can offer you companionship and affection."

And Adam didn't have that in him. Never had, never would.

Julie hadn't seen or heard from Adam in the past six days, although there was a good reason for that. She'd avoided Kidville on Wednesday, his usual day to volunteer. Still, he had her number and could've called if he'd wanted to.

At first she'd been happy that he hadn't, but by the time Friday rolled around, she found herself checking her cell phone for missed calls. It had become an annoying habit, and she looked one more time before getting out of her car and heading to the classroom, where she was providing a music therapy session.

Thirty minutes later, as Julie put away her guitar, as well as the tambourines, maracas and kazoos, she decided to stick around for a while. Since there was zero parental involvement with school activities, there never seemed to be enough adult hands. So there always seemed to be a list of things to do.

Before she could offer her help, the teacher approached. "You're amazing, Julie. The kids love you, and so do I."

"I'm glad. It's fun to see the children respond to music. And I enjoy working with them, even when I'm not playing the guitar or singing." Julie tucked a loose strand of hair behind her ear. "In fact, I don't have anything planned this afternoon, so if there's something I can help you do, just let me know."

"Actually," Mrs. Wright said, "I'm glad to hear that. I'm supposed to meet with Donna and Ms. Kincaid, Eddie and Cassie's social worker. Jim will cover for me, but it might be best to separate the kids during art. Would you mind supervising the younger ones while they finger-paint?"

"No problem. That sounds simple enough. But..." Julie bit down on her bottom lip. "This probably isn't any of my business, but what's that meeting about?"

"Ms. Kincaid thinks the children would be better off living with a family, rather than in a group home. And the Hoffmans and I disagree."

"I do, too. They're doing so well here." And if they left and went somewhere else, Julie would lose contact with them. "I'm sure Ms. Kincaid will value your opinion."

"I'm not so sure about that," Karen said. "She's pretty strict and a bit cynical for a woman who's supposed to look out for a child's best interests."

"What do you mean?"

"She's not a bad person, but she's got some strong ideas about what children need. And in my opinion, they're pretty outdated. Hopefully, she'll retire soon."

"But maybe not soon enough."

"Actually," Karen said, "from what I heard, that day *is* coming fairly soon, and she's determined to go out as a shining star when it comes to placing the remaining children on her caseload."

"If she's insistent or headstrong about putting Eddie and Cassie in a real home, I just might offer to take them myself." The words rolled off Julie's tongue without a thought, but the idea wasn't half-bad. In fact, she rather liked the sound of that option, although it would change her life dramatically.

Still, she'd grown fond of Eddie and Cassie. And maybe, if she could provide a better life for them, any changes she had to make would be worth it.

Ten minutes later, Julie was seated on a child-size chair, overseeing five children in the art room.

Cassie sat at Julie's right, and Mason, a mischievous red-haired six-year-old, was to her left, his hands a green mess.

"I need more paint," Mason said.

He clearly had plenty, but since he seemed to be tapping into his creative side and having fun as he did, Julie took the plastic container and squirted another glob onto his paper.

Unlike Mason, Cassie was hesitant to get her hands dirty.

"Don't worry," Julie told the timid little girl, "the

paint washes off easily. And it won't stain your clothes. Just smoosh it around with your fingers." She watched for a moment as Cassie tentatively used her index finger and made a blue streak. "That's it, honey. There you go."

While the kids worked, Julie reached into her purse, which she'd set under the table, removed her iPhone and checked for missed calls. Nope. Still nothing.

Oh, for Pete's sake. Get a grip. She shoved the cell back where it belonged.

What was the matter with her? The guy was so not her type. And he certainly wasn't worth stressing over. She suspected he had a variety of attractive women coming in and out of his life as if passing through a revolving door. And Julie wasn't up for a casual fling.

As the door squeaked open, she glanced up, expecting to see either Karen or one of the Hoffmans. Instead, she spotted Adam, who was dressed casually in a light blue button-down shirt, the sleeves rolled up, and black jeans. When he flashed a heart-stopping grin, her breath caught.

He crossed the room and approached the table, his gorgeous brown eyes zeroing in on her.

"What a…surprise," she said, doing her best to conjure an unaffected smile. But the biggest surprise was that she'd actually been able to form a greeting at all.

He gazed at the messy table and gooey hands. "Wow. Look at all those amazing colors."

Cassie, whose hands were only a bit blue, used her forearm to swipe at a loose strand of hair from her face. As far as Julie knew, the little girl had yet to talk to anyone, but she no longer clung to her brother when they were separated for different art projects. And during music, she smiled whenever the other children sang silly songs.

Adam knelt beside Cassie, taking an interest in her and her artwork. But Julie couldn't blame him. She was drawn to the doe-eyed child, too.

"I like your picture," Adam told Cassie.

"Then you should see mine!" Mason called out. "Cassie's paper is mostly still clean and white, but look at all the green I used."

"Very nice," Julie told the boy who'd managed to get paint on his arms, nearly up to the elbows. "I like both pictures. Everyone is doing a super job—no matter how much paint they use."

As the children continued to swirl their hands through the paint, Adam turned to Julie. "Can I talk to you for a minute?" He nodded toward the sink.

What do you want to talk about? she nearly asked. Instead, she pushed back the small chair on which she'd been seated and got to her feet, both eager and reluctant to hear what he had to say.

Adam led her to the area where the kids would wash up later, then he lowered his voice to a whisper. "Is Cassie talking yet?"

"No," Julie said. "Not as far as I know. But she responds silently to instructions. And she's obedient. I think she's coming along. She's even smiled a couple of times."

"That sounds like a step in the right direction. She's

probably afraid to do something wrong and get in trouble. Brady had a real mean streak, and she may not have known when to expect a smack in the head."

Julie winced. "That breaks my heart."

They stood like that for several beats, side by side, gazing at Cassie, who seemed more afraid than reluctant to get her hands dirty.

"How's Eddie doing?" Adam asked.

"All right, but he's been leery of letting Cassie out of his sight."

"Yeah, I figured. He's been her only protector for nearly a year. Maybe more."

Julie knew what it felt like to be someone's only protector. But it felt even worse when you realized that you'd failed.

"Have you had any luck in finding their mother?" she asked.

"Not yet. But I have a feeling she didn't leave on her own volition. I'm going to ask Jim about getting a sample of the kids' DNA to compare to any Jane Does in the morgue."

"Their situation is so sad. But at least they know they're both safe here."

"I knew that would happen, and I'm glad. But I'd feel a lot better if Cassie would start talking."

"Me, too. Jim discussed her situation with the child psychologist, and Dr. Wang told him to give Cassie more time."

Adam nodded, but his eyes remained focused on

the little girl. He seemed genuinely concerned. Maybe that's why he'd dropped by Kidville today.

As silly as it was, and as much as Julie hated to admit it, she had hoped that he'd come to see *her*.

"I thought you worked with Jesse on Wednesdays," she said.

"Yes, but I've been working overtime this week and missed, so I came to see him today. But I wanted to check on Cassie and Eddie first. After that, I'll take Jesse for an ice cream."

"I'll bet Cassie and Eddie would like to join you guys."

"They have ice cream almost every night for dessert."

"I wasn't talking about getting a treat. I meant they'd probably enjoy spending time with you."

"Oh." He shrugged. "Yeah, you're probably right. But I'm making some real headway with Jesse. And so far, I've made it a point to mentor one kid at a time."

She wondered if he had the same philosophy when it came to his dating life—just one woman at a time. But she kept her curiosity at bay.

"It's probably time to help those kids clean up," she said, although she felt inclined to keep talking to Adam.

He followed her to the table, which by now was a real mess. And so were the kids. That is, all but Cassie, who was studying her blue palms and fingertips with a scrunched brow.

"I just thought of something I need to do to finish

my picture," Mason said, his eyes bright, his smile contagious. "Can you give me a squidge more paint?"

Against her better judgment, Julie squirted one last green glob on his paper. Before she could turn away, he smacked his artwork, leaving his handprint and splattering paint in all directions, including Julie's face.

"All done!" Mason said. When he looked up at Julie, his jaw dropped and his eyes opened wide. "I'm sorry."

Julie didn't need a mirror to know she was adorned with an array of green freckles.

Cassie appeared terrified, as if she knew all hell was about to break loose.

When Adam laughed, breaking the tension in the room, Julie laughed, too. "Now I look like a green-speckled frog."

Mason chuckled. "Yeah, you do. Just like the one in that song you sang with us."

"I'll bet," she said. "Maybe next time we should have art first, then music. That way my croaks will be more realistic."

"I've always liked frogs and toads," Adam said, his gorgeous brown eyes glimmering as he chuckled once more.

Julie glanced at Cassie, who appeared to be more curious now than frightened.

"I think Miss Julie makes a pretty frog," Adam added.

Oh, yeah? A smug smile stretched across Julie's face, as she reached into Mason's paint with her index finger then smeared a line across Adam's brow.

"Hey," he said.

Unable to leave her artwork undone, she turned the line into a Z—for *Zorro*.

Adam placed his hands on his hips, but his expression wasn't the least bit stern. "I might have to arrest you for defacing a police officer."

"I don't think that charge would hold up in court." She winked at him, then glanced at the giggling children. Even Cassie had joined in, wearing a great big smile, the biggest Julie had ever seen.

"Let's get these little rugrats cleaned up before we all get in trouble," Adam said.

Several minutes later, the kids' hands were spick-and-span. Their clothes? Not so much.

When the art room door squeaked open, Mrs. Wright entered the room. She glanced first at the messy table and paint-splattered floor, then at the adults who'd been supervising the kids. "Oh, my. Don't tell me. A paint fight?"

Julie smiled. "I guess you could say that."

"Why don't I take the children outside for recess," the teacher said, clearly fighting a smile. "Then maybe the two of you can…settle your differences." She chuckled as she herded the kids outdoors, leaving Adam and Julie to wash up.

Instead, they merely stood there, studying each other. They seemed to be at a loss for words. At least Julie was.

Finally, Adam said, "I'm sorry for laughing, but you have to admit, it was pretty funny."

"I know. And when Cassie actually giggled, I decided to get even sillier. It was a huge relief to see her open up."

"Sometimes, letting loose and being playful is a good thing. It's actually therapeutic. Like music."

He had a point.

"So what do police officers do for fun?" she asked.

"We have paintball fights." He laughed, then turned on the water, dampened a paper towel and turned toward her.

She reached to take the paper towel from him, but he stopped her. "Here. Let me."

In spite of all the convincing self-talk she'd had after he canceled their plans on Saturday night, she lowered her arm.

As Adam gently wiped the green splatters, his movements slow and steady, he cupped her jaw with his left hand, his fingers stretching dangerously close to the sensitive soft spot behind her ear. Her cheeks heated, and her skin tingled at his touch.

He wasn't just wiping her face, he was stirring her senses and making a simple touch into something akin to foreplay.

But dang. That's exactly what this was—at least, as far as she was concerned. Before her knees buckled, revealing her weakness for him, she cleared her throat and took a step back. "Thanks. I'm sure you got it all. Besides, I need to get this room cleaned up so I can go outside and help supervise the kids on the playground."

She expected to see a cocky grin stretched across his face, but his expression was serious, his gaze heated.

She could only speculate on what he might be thinking, but she'd rather not go there.

Thankfully, he didn't comment, which was just as well. Talk about opening a Pandora's box of trouble.

Julie had dreamed of finding a special man to love, but Adam Santiago wasn't that guy, no matter how hot he was, how dazzling his smile. Of that, she was sure.

Now all she had to do was convince her raging hormones.

Chapter Five

Last Friday, when Julie had been within arm's reach, Adam had been just one heartbeat away from kissing her, and a breath away from asking her out. Fortunately, he'd frozen up and did neither.

Despite being a guy who'd been awarded several commendations for his courage under fire, he morphed into a wimp when he was with Julie. She scared him. Or rather, to be more accurate, he scared himself.

He'd never felt so conflicted over a woman, and he'd experienced more than his share of relationships—if you could call them that.

But Julie wasn't like the others. She was a novelty, a complete puzzle that he felt compelled to solve. And there lay the problem. She was the kind of woman who deserved more from a relationship than a good time, great sex and an amazing afterglow, which was all Adam would ever be able to give her.

Only trouble was, he was so tempted to kiss her that the next time he had the chance, he might not be able to resist. For that reason, he'd decided to keep his distance before he did or said something stupid.

But that plan fell apart when he stopped by Kidville on Monday afternoon. He told himself the unexpected visit would give him the opportunity to check on Cassie and Eddie, to see how the kids were doing. And although that was certainly a concern, there was more to it.

How much more, he couldn't say. All he knew was that the Bronco seemed to have driven itself to the children's home, and he hadn't done a damned thing to alter the route.

So what if he felt drawn to Julie? What was wrong with enjoying her company?

After parking, Adam headed toward the classroom located in the red schoolhouse. Just as he reached the front door, Karen stepped outside, followed by a line of children.

"Jesse's not here," Karen told him, obviously assuming he'd come to see the boy he'd been mentoring.

Adam didn't correct her. "Where is he?"

"Having a play date with his younger brother. He's been doing much better since you took him under your wing, so we thought it was time to test the waters."

"I came to the same conclusion, so I'm glad to hear that." Adam made a quick scan of the kids, realizing only half of them were with the teacher. "Where's everyone else?"

"I'm taking the second and third graders out for PE," she said. "You're welcome to join us for a game of kickball on the playground, unless you'd rather help with a beadwork project."

It shouldn't be a tough decision. Hell, Adam was far more interested in sports than art. But Julie was probably supervising the younger kids with that craft project.

"I'd like to visit Eddie and Cassie while I'm here, so I'll head over to the art room."

"Great." She studied him a moment. "This isn't your normal day to visit us."

"You're right. But whenever I work over the weekend, they give me extra time off."

"It's nice that you want to spend those days with us."

Tell that to his buddies, Clay and Matt, who'd started to complain that he didn't have time for them.

Karen offered him a smile before leading the older kids out to the ball field.

Adam crossed the yard and entered the art room, where Julie and her younger charges were stringing brightly colored beads on strings of red yarn. A basket containing a roll of yarn, a pair of scissors and a plastic bag of extra beads sat on the rectangular table.

He suspected they were nearly finished, although it would take some time to pick up all the beads that had fallen to the floor.

Julie glanced up from her project, caught his eye and dazzled him with a dimpled grin. "What a surprise. You're just in time to see the necklaces we made."

"Very nice," he said. "Pretty, in fact." But he wasn't just talking about the beads they'd strung.

Each time he saw Julie, even today, when she'd dressed casually in a pale yellow long-sleeve T-shirt, blue jeans and a pair of sneakers, he found her more and more attractive. In fact, he no longer had to envision her dressed in a fancy red cocktail dress to spark a sexual fantasy.

Julie scooted back the small chair upon which she was sitting, got to her feet and approached Adam holding the necklace she'd made. "Let's try this on for size."

Adam might have objected and refused to let her put it around his neck, but when the children giggled at Julie's silly antics, especially Cassie, who found it especially funny, he went along with it.

"Perfect," she said as she adjusted it, her hands lingering on his shoulders, her citrusy scent taunting him. "I made it just for you."

He doubted that, but he thanked her just the same.

"All right, kids." Julie turned around to face the children. "Let's pick up our mess so we can go out to the playground."

"Are we going to play freeze tag again?" Mason asked. "It was fun yesterday."

"I don't see why not." Julie glanced at Adam. "Are you up for a fast-paced game?"

"Always." He winked, and his lips quirked in a crooked grin.

If she had any idea what he was thinking, she didn't let on. Instead, she encouraged the children to clean up. "Mason and Eddie, I'd like you to pick up the beads on the floor."

Eager to please, Eddie dropped to his knees and got busy. Mason, who'd scrunched his face when he heard his assignment, blew out a sigh and reached for the basket on the table.

"Here," he told Eddie. "Put them back in the bag." As he swung around to hand the basket to Eddie, he lost his grip and it fell to the floor, spilling its contents.

Beads flew every which way, bouncing and skidding and rolling, until they had a real mess on their hands.

Mason gasped. "It was an accident. I was just trying to help. I'm sorry."

"I know, Mason. I'll help you pick them up." Julie avoided several of the plastic balls on the floor, only to fail to notice a few others. When she stepped on then, she lost her footing. "Oops."

Adam reached out to grab her, hoping he could stop her from falling, but his efforts knocked him off balance, and they both took a hard tumble. He did his best to protect her as they fell, his shoulder taking the brunt of it when they landed on the floor.

"Are you okay?" he asked, as he continued to hold her.

"I think so." She didn't move. She merely stared at him, as if she was afraid to shift her weight and end the awkward embrace.

But he didn't care. It felt good to hold her close, to smell the citrusy scent of her shampoo. And he didn't give a rip that they had a pint-size audience looking on.

Mason began to sing, "Julie and Adam, sitting in a tree…"

Adam was familiar with the playground ditty. And he was tempted to wrap up the show by K-I-S-S-I-N-G Julie senseless. In fact, he almost did just that, when the door squeaked open and footsteps sounded, telling him the audience had grown.

"My goodness!" Karen called out. "What in the world happened?"

"It was his fault." Mason pointed at Adam. "He knocked Miss Julie down and wouldn't let her get up, even when she said she was okay."

"Actually," Adam said, as he slowly got to his feet, avoiding any stray beads that might unbalance him again, "I was trying to keep Miss Julie from falling, but it didn't work very well." He reached for Julie's hand to help her up.

Again, the children giggled, but Julie didn't find the situation the least bit funny. She might have lost her footing when she stepped on a couple of beads, but she faced an even bigger risk of falling hard and getting hurt if she were to act on her growing attraction to Adam.

Still, when she took the hand he offered her, her breath caught. His palm was warm, his fingers long, his grip strong. And while she was upright once again, she didn't feel the least bit steady.

"Why don't you two take the children out to the playground?" Karen asked. "I'd hate for one of them to slip and fall. I'll clean up this mess."

"No," Julie said. "I'll do that. You and Mr. Adam can

take them out." That would give her the opportunity to ponder what she was feeling, what she was sensing.

She felt a tug on the hem of her T-shirt and looked down to see Cassie gazing up at her. "I... I'll help you."

At the sound of that sweet little voice, Julie nearly dropped to the floor once again. Had the words come from any other child, Julie would have thanked her for the offer and sent her out to play. But there was no way she would refuse Cassie. Not when those were the very first words she'd spoken since Adam had brought her and her brother to Kidville.

"Thanks," Julie told the girl. "I'd really appreciate your help, honey. But promise me you'll be careful not to step on any beads. I don't want you to get hurt."

Cassie brightened, clearly delighted to have such an important job to do, then she dropped to her knees and began picking up stray beads.

"Since Miss Julie already has someone to help her pick up the mess," Adam said, "let's go out to the playground."

"Mr. Hoffman is supervising the kickball game," Karen said. "Tell him I'll relieve him in a couple of minutes."

Moments later, when Julie and Cassie had the mess cleaned up, Karen said, "You two make a good team."

"Yes, we do." Julie placed a hand on Cassie's small shoulder and gave it a gentle squeeze. "I'm so glad you offered to give up some of your recess time, honey. You were a huge help. Why don't you go on out and play?"

Cassie smiled, clearly pleased to have been useful,

then she hurried out the door. Once she was outside, Karen said, "You and Adam make a good team, too."

Julie wanted to argue, but she couldn't. In spite of all her reservations about the guy, that seemed to be true.

"I can hardly believe it," Karen said. "You were the first one who was able to get through to Cassie. She finally opened up and spoke. And I couldn't be happier."

"Me, too."

"I talked to Jamison, the counselor on staff. She's been working with Eddie and Cassie. Apparently, she talked to Eddie about his sister's silence, and he told her that Cassie used to talk all the time. But one day, Brady, the man they'd been living with, smacked her in the face and told her to shut up. Then he threatened to knock her head off if she opened her mouth again. It seems she took the threat seriously."

"I'm sure she did." Julie blew out a sigh. "From what I heard, the man was a brute—and maybe a murderer. I hope he stays in jail for a long time."

"So do I," Karen said. "Ms. Kincaid, Eddie and Cassie's social worker, is looking for the perfect placement for them."

"I'm not sure why she doesn't realize this is the best place for them to be."

"I agree with you, but Ms. Kincaid isn't convinced that our program will work, especially for them. She thinks they should have an actual family experience so they'll know what one is really like. That way, when they grow up, they'll be able to have a loving, stable home of their own."

Julie could understand the reasoning, but didn't

Ms. Kincaid realize that the kids were happy here, that they'd begun to bond with the Hoffmans, their teacher...and Julie?

"Apparently," Karen said, "the kids have relatives who have come forward to take them, but they're questionable, as far as I'm concerned."

Karen nodded to the door. "Come on, I'll explain while we go outside. I need to supervise recess."

Julie followed her out, but before she could get more than a few of her mounting questions answered, a loud spat broke out on the handball court. Two boys disagreed about whose turn came next, and it looked as if they planned to slug it out.

Karen blew the whistle she wore around her neck and headed toward them before things could get out of hand. "That'll be enough, you two."

Adam, who'd been talking to Eddie near the slide, laughed at something the boy said, then turned and walked away.

Julie watched his approach, noting his sexy swagger and his heart-strumming smile.

"I never used to feel sorry for teachers when I was a kid," Adam said. "But damn. I had no idea how tough their jobs were."

Julie offered him a smile. "You're right. But it can be rewarding, too. Like today, when Cassie spoke for the first time."

"I know. That was cool. She really seems to have taken a liking to you."

Julie'd noticed that, too. "Just so you know," she said, tapping the handmade necklace Adam still wore, "that's why I placed those beads around your neck. And that's also why I painted the *Z* on your face the other day. I like hearing children laugh, especially Cassie. And I decided it would be fun to stretch things out a bit."

Adam chuckled. "I didn't know it before, but you have a playful side I hadn't expected."

"You're right. It's hard not to when you're a music therapist who sings silly songs and dances with children. But sometimes, like today, you just have to put on a happy face and pretend everything is going to be all right."

He studied her for a moment, as if trying to process her comment. When he finally spoke, it was a question. "What's wrong?"

She sighed. "Karen just gave me some unsettling news. Apparently, Eddie and Cassie have some relatives who mentioned that they could take them."

"Wouldn't it be better for them to be with members of their own family?"

"You'd think so. But…" Julie sucked in a breath, then let it out in a jagged huff. "From what I understand, the couple is a little…sketchy."

"What's that mean?"

"I'm not sure. But apparently, their maternal uncle is a friend of the guy they'd been living with."

"Brady Thatcher? Their mother's boyfriend who was in jail for child abuse? That isn't a good sign of their character."

"Neither is the fact that they asked what the state paid foster parents these days."

"You got that right."

"For that reason," Julie said, "I'm going to offer to take both kids."

"Really?" Adam looked surprised. "That's a big step."

"And one that might not pan out. Ms. Kincaid believes the kids would be better off with a married couple."

"In this day and age?" Adam slowly shook his head. "What are the chances that Jim can put the woman off until after she retires? In fact, he might be able to get the counselor at Kidville to intervene."

"That's the plan."

"It sounds like a good one to me."

Julie lifted her hand and crossed her fingers. "I just hope it works."

"Me, too."

Julie bit down on her bottom lip, worried that things wouldn't work out the way she wanted them to.

"Hey," Adam said, "Just so you know, I'll get the names of that couple and run a background check on them."

"Thanks. I hoped you'd say that."

"If they're as sketchy as Karen thinks, they might have a criminal background. And if they do, that might solve all your problems."

"One way or another, I suppose."

He studied her again, his gaze intense. Then his expression softened, and his brown eyes glimmered. "Should we try for dinner again on Friday night?"

There it was. The invitation Julie had been prepared for, yet for some breathless reason, every response she'd rehearsed while playing out imaginary conversations in her mind whooshed out of her. Gone.

"Sure," she said. "Why not?"

"Good. I'll pick you up at your house at six o'clock."

As he turned to go, she said, "Call me beforehand and I'll give you my address. You have my number." And she wasn't just talking about her phone.

On Tuesday, Julie decided to clean out both the closet and the dresser in the spare bedroom to make room for the kids. Her plan might not work, but that didn't mean she couldn't show the social worker that she was ready for them, that she was able to provide for their needs and comfort.

She'd no more than headed down the hall with a plastic trash bag and an empty box when her stomach growled. And before she could even think about taking a lunch break, her cell phone rang. When she glanced at the display, she didn't recognize the number. But she answered anyway. "Hello?"

"It's Adam."

"Where are you?" she asked.

"Police headquarters. Can you meet me for a quick lunch at La Cocina, the Mexican restaurant in town?"

A date? Even a quick one sounded great. "Sure, I can meet you there."

"I have something I want to tell you."

So not a date?

"I ran a background check on Vivian and Larry

Stanford," he said, "the shirttail relatives interested in providing Cassie and Eddie a home."

"What'd you find out?"

"Karen was right. They're pretty sketchy. I don't have time to go into it now. I'll talk to you at lunch. Is one o'clock too late?"

"No, I'll be there."

In fact, she was so eager to hear what he had to say that she arrived early.

Twenty minutes later, she was sitting at a red wooden table at La Cocina, munching on chips and salsa while waiting for Adam, who was running late for their lunch date.

She studied the interior of the quaint Mexican restaurant, particularly a mural of mariachis serenading a lovely senorita. The other white plastered walls were adorned with colorful southwestern blankets, a few black sombreros and several antique frames displaying photographs that had been taken in the early part of the last century.

She'd just reached for another chip when she spotted Adam coming through the door. She waved, and he made his way toward her.

"I'm sorry I'm late."

"No problem," she said.

A hank of dark hair had flopped onto his brow, and a serious expression suggested that he'd rushed from the parking lot. "How long have you been waiting?"

"Not long," she said.

He glanced down at the half-eaten basket of chips, then arched a single brow, clearly doubting her words.

"Okay, I stretched the truth a tad. I got here early, but I really didn't mind the wait."

He flashed a dazzling smile, morphing into the charming and handsome guy she'd been expecting to see. He pulled out a bulky red chair, the legs scraping the floor, and took the seat across from hers. "I'm afraid I'm going to have to cut out early. I have to get back to headquarters for a meeting."

Okay, so this wasn't an actual date. She could deal with that, but she'd skipped breakfast and was starving, which was why more than half the tortilla chips were already gone.

"Do you have time to eat something?" she asked. Not that she was uncomfortable going to restaurants on her own, but—date or no date—she'd been looking forward to seeing him again.

"I'll probably just get a *carne asada* burrito to go and pay our tab as soon as we order." He motioned for the waitress, a matronly woman with dark hair, rosy cheeks and a friendly smile.

If he didn't consider this a date, she certainly wasn't going to let him think she'd made that jump. "Let's ask for separate tabs."

"No way," he said. "I got this."

After they placed their orders, Julie leaned forward, her forearms resting on the edge of the table. "So what'd you find out about the Stanfords?"

"Well, they aren't exactly hardened criminals." He reached for a chip and dipped it into the salsa. "But they're definitely what I'd call sketchy."

"What do you mean by that?"

"They both have quite a few court records," he said. "Vivian had a stack of unpaid parking tickets, and there was a warrant out for her arrest. She's now on a payment plan. Last year, she was charged with disturbing the peace. Apparently, she had an argument with a neighbor that turned into a shouting match. And after she made threats, the neighbor filed a restraining order against her."

"She doesn't sound like she'd make a good foster mother," Julie said.

"I agree. She'd make a crappy role model, too."

Julie hoped that Ms. Kincaid would agree, but who knew what she'd say.

"As for Larry Stanford, he has a couple of DUIs, the most recent in February of last year. He spent time in jail for that one and had his license revoked. He's supposed to attend AA meetings, although I haven't had a chance to talk to his probation officer yet."

As much as Julie hoped the news Adam had uncovered might affect Ms. Kincaid's decision, she had a feeling the social worker would say Mr. Stanford had paid his debt to society and that he was doing his best to turn his life around.

"I also ran a credit check," Adam said. "Vivian and Larry aren't exactly up to their eyeballs in debt, but they're definitely having financial trouble."

"Since they asked how much they'd receive as foster parents, I think that money is their primary motivation."

"I agree."

The waitress arrived with a bowl of tortilla soup,

a white paper bag with the burrito and the bill. Adam whipped out his credit card and handed it to her. Not wanting to be overheard, Julie ate in silence until she walked away.

"I'm not sure if I uncovered anything that would prevent an old-fashioned social worker from granting them custody," Adam said.

Julie wanted to argue, but he was right. In her heart, she knew the Stanfords couldn't provide a proper home for the kids, but she had a feeling Ms. Kincaid wouldn't see things that way.

"I'm sorry," Adam said. "I wish I had better news."

Julie pushed aside her half-eaten bowl of tortilla soup, no longer hungry—and not just because of the chips she'd eaten earlier.

"If it makes you feel any better," Adam added, "I'm worried about those kids, too."

That didn't make her feel the least bit better because he obviously knew things could go badly for Eddie and Cassie, and there wasn't a darn thing either of them could do about it.

"I spoke to Jim about Ms. Kincaid this morning," Adam said. "According to him, she thinks Cassie would do better if she wasn't in such a large group setting. And she'd like to get them into an actual foster home as soon as possible."

"I offered to take the kids myself," Julie said.

"That would be nice—if it works out."

"Yes, but I don't know… Ms. Kincaid is… Well, she seems pretty conservative." Julie blew out a weary sigh. "She has some strong opinions, even if they're outdated. And something tells me she's not going to give a rip about parking tickets or neighborhood altercations or…even past DUIs." Just that possibility triggered a ripple of nausea, and Julie took a sip of water, hoping to wash it away.

"Keep in mind," Adam said, "in this day and age, the court won't necessarily agree with her."

"You might be right, but Ms. Kincaid is so well-respected, the court might allow the Stanfords to foster the kids on her say-so alone. It's just too bad I'm not married. Then I'd have a fighting chance of getting custody."

They sat in silence for a moment. Julie suspected Adam was trying to wrap his mind around the situation, just as she was.

"How soon will the decision will be made?" Adam asked.

"Ms. Kincaid is supposed to retire in a couple of weeks, and Jim told me she was determined to find placements for all the children on her caseload by then." Julie lifted her glass and took another sip of water, which didn't seem to settle her queasy stomach. Then she blew out a sigh. "I wish that woman didn't have a thing against single parents, but I can't be something I'm not."

"No guy in sight?" Adam asked.

Actually, a very tempting guy sat across the table from her right now, gripping that paper bag that held his lunch as if he was about to make a mad dash out of the restaurant. But there was no way she'd admit that, even if this had turned out to be a real date, which it clearly hadn't.

"No," she said, "I'm not dating anyone at the moment. But maybe I can convince Ms. Kincaid that she's wrong about single parents. My dad was in the military and deployed a lot, so my mother pretty much raised me alone. And she was a great mom. We were really close."

As she lifted her glass to take another drink, Adam got to his feet and said, "I have to run, but a weird thought just crossed my mind."

At this point, she'd consider wild ideas. "Okay, let's hear it."

"What if we got married?"

Chapter Six

Julie choked on the water she'd tried to swallow and sputtered, "Are you kidding?"

"I haven't actually thought it out, so I'm grasping at straws. But what I'm suggesting wouldn't be a real marriage."

"That sounds fraudulent."

"Maybe so, but no one would need to know about the plan except us. Then, after you're awarded custody of the kids, we could file for an annulment. By then, the social worker would have retired." Adam blew out a sigh of his own. "It sounds desperate, I know. But I'd do just about anything to make sure those kids have a good, safe and loving home. And in my opinion, the best one would be yours." He nodded to the front entrance. "I have to run, but think it over. We can talk more later."

Stunned by the sudden…proposal, Julie merely nodded and watched Adam hurry out of the restaurant.

A marriage was certainly more serious than a date, and even though Julie was stunned by Adam's suggestion, she was touched by it, too.

She hadn't known him very long, and while her admiration for and attraction to him was growing deeper each day, his plan was a real stretch.

She'd never marry anyone unless the man she loved felt the same way about her. And her feelings for Adam ran deep. In fact, she could easily fall head over heels for him, if she hadn't already. But she doubted Adam felt the same way about her.

Pride urged her to not give Adam's suggestion another thought.

But what about Eddie and Cassie?

In all honesty, she'd do anything to keep those kids safe. On top of that, she'd come to believe that Adam could be the man she'd been waiting for all her life. He might not be in love with her now, but maybe, given time, his feelings for her would grow.

Hey, it happened in books and movies all the time.

As she pushed back her chair and stood, she made a decision she could live with.

If Adam brought it up again, she'd agree to his plan. But maybe he'd have a change of heart after he had a chance to think on it.

As Adam climbed into the government-issued vehicle he'd driven to La Cocina, he swore under his breath. He rarely spoke without thinking, but the words had rolled off his tongue before he could stop them. And he had no excuse for it.

The idea of a marriage on paper wasn't necessarily a bad one, considering their motives, and it would probably work. But then what?

Just the thought of getting married, even if it was only temporary, scared the crap out of him.

But so did the idea of that social worker clinging to her old-style beliefs and sending those kids to live with guardians who could turn out to be worse than Brady Thatcher.

And with their mother out of the picture—not that Adam believed that cock-and-bull story Brady had told them about her running off to Hollywood—the Stanfords were the only family they had left.

Adam had tried to find their mom, like he'd promised. But so far, he hadn't had any luck. Since he suspected foul play, he'd talked to Jim and Donna, who approved of him taking DNA samples from the kids. The plan was to match them against the databases of any unidentified females who'd been dead for a year or so. If things turned out the way he thought they would, that would leave Eddie and Cassie orphaned.

He pondered the idea of a fake marriage for the rest of the day, which distracted him several times during an unexpected stakeout that night. It had also lingered in his mind until he parked in front of his house just before dawn.

As he unlocked the front door, a bark sounded. Apparently, the scaredy-cat was becoming a watchdog. How about that?

"It's me," he said as he let himself inside.

The dog greeted him at the door with little woofs and a wagging tail. He bent to greet her with a caress of her shaggy head. "Are you glad to see me, girl?"

Another bark said she was. And that made him glad, too.

She was really coming around, and he was glad. Who knew what abuse she'd gone through while out on the streets? Oddly enough, she hadn't been leery of Eddie and Cassie when Adam had found them together. Maybe she'd sensed that those two had been just as traumatized by cruelty as she'd been.

Adam scratched behind her ear, and she tilted her head to give him better access, her tail thumping upon the floor. Then, as was their habit, he rewarded her with another treat. And as usual, she gobbled it up.

He laughed. "I wasn't going to name you, but I think Biscuit would be a good one."

She sat on her haunches, her wagging tail sweeping the floor.

"Then Biscuit it is."

Just like the dog, Eddie and Cassie seemed to be coming along, too. They were especially responsive to Julie. But hell, how could they not be? Even Adam found himself lowering his guard around her.

Would Biscuit respond to Julie in a similar way? Would her music and songs lull the skittish little thing into a peaceful, trusting state?

Maybe he should invite her over one evening and find out.

As he made his way to the kitchen, Biscuit coming

along with him, he said, "You'll never guess what I got us into today."

Biscuit pranced at his side as if she didn't care what he'd done. She'd follow him anywhere.

He smiled. He'd always admired loyalty and trust.

After preparing Biscuit's food and refreshing the water in her bowl, he glanced at Stan's answering machine, its red light blinking.

That was odd. Most of his friends already knew Stan had died. It was probably just a sales call.

He shook it off and went back to pondering his offer to marry Julie, which ought to make him head for the hills.

It didn't, though. As time went by, his uneasiness about marriage, especially one that was only on paper, had dissipated. And as he'd said, they could get an annulment later.

He glanced at the clock on the microwave. It was pretty late to be calling Julie, but they didn't have much time to waste.

Ms. Kincaid is supposed to retire in a couple of weeks, Julie had said.

And according to Jim Hoffman, the social worker was dead set on placing those kids in a home by then. So time was running out.

He reached for his cell and dialed Julie's number. If she'd come up with a better idea than his, he'd like to hear it.

Julie had just placed a bookmark in the novel she'd been reading and turned out the light on her nightstand when her cell phone rang. "Hey," Adam said. "I hope I didn't wake you."

"No, I'm still up." But had he called five minutes later that wouldn't have been the case. She turned on the bedside lamp, then flung off the blanket and sat on the edge of the bed.

"Have you had a chance to think over that plan?" he asked.

That's about all she'd been able to do, although she'd finally decided to read so she could focus on something else and, hopefully, get a good night's sleep.

"Yes," she admitted. "I've given it some thought."

"And…?"

"If you're willing, I am." Just to make sure he didn't think she expected their marriage to be real, she added, "It's possible that all we need to do is let Ms. Kincaid think we're getting married. Maybe announcing our engagement would be enough to sway her."

"It's possible," Adam said, "but I have a feeling she's going to expect us to be legally married and have a household that's already set up for the kids."

"I don't like the idea of lying, but what if you moved in with me for a while, and we just told her we were married?"

"That's not going to fly. She works for the county, so it'd be too easy for her check out the records. Besides, I've learned that it's better to be honest. It makes the story you tell easier to remember."

Gosh, she loved that. Honesty was important in a relationship—even though she had no idea what he expected from the one that was budding between them.

"So where do we go from here?" she asked.

"The best and fastest thing to do would be to be married by a justice of the peace at the courthouse as soon as possible."

She'd always envisioned a church wedding, but this one wouldn't be real, even if she hoped that Adam's feelings for her might blossom into love.

"All right," she said. "When do you think we should do this?"

"The sooner, the better. How about Thursday afternoon?"

Wow. The day after tomorrow? Things were moving along so...fast. But if they intended to convince Ms. Kincaid that the kids would be better off with her than with the Stanfords, they didn't have time to drag their feet.

"Sure," she said. "I can meet you there."

"Great. Now all we have to do is decide on a honeymoon."

Her breath caught. "Seriously?"

"Are you opposed?"

She got to her feet and began to pace the darkened bedroom, trying to wrap her mind around it all. "Do you think we should actually...go someplace?"

"It would be more convincing."

Maybe so. Was he suggesting that they should also experience all that went with a honeymoon? That idea both stunned and excited her.

"That sounds nice," she said, "but we should keep in mind that we can only get an annulment if the marriage isn't consummated."

"Whether it is or not, who'd know the difference?"

Heat flooded her cheeks, her heart spun in her chest and nervous anticipation stirred up an ache in her core. Thank goodness they weren't talking face-to-face. She'd hate for him to know how tempted she was to...

She returned to the bed and took a seat on the edge of the mattress. "I suppose no one would know."

He paused a couple of beats. "We can talk about the perks of a paper marriage later. I'll meet you on the courthouse steps at one o'clock."

"All right." She glanced at the clock on the bureau. In less than forty-eight hours she'd be a bride. And while the wedding wasn't going to be anything like the one she'd once dreamed about as a girl, she couldn't help looking forward to meeting him—and seeing how their honeymoon played out.

Just thinking about kissing Adam convinced her that it might be impossible to resist those "perks."

By the time one o'clock on Thursday had rolled around, Adam had taken a leave of absence. He'd also told Jim Hoffman that he and Julie were getting married, an announcement that had pleased the man to no end.

"I'll call Ms. Kincaid with the good news," Jim said. "And I'll follow up by emailing her a letter of recommendation for her files. Hopefully, that'll be enough to convince her that Eddie and Cassie should be placed with you and Julie—and that you'll both provide them with a loving home."

Actually, Adam hadn't planned to move into Julie's

house. The kids would live with her, and she'd be creating that home. But that was their secret. Once Ms. Kincaid retired, it wouldn't matter anymore.

After talking to Jim, he called his sergeant and let her know that he needed to take a few days off—in case he and Julie decided to take that honeymoon.

A smile stretched across his lips. He'd only been teasing her when he first brought up the subject, but she'd taken him seriously, which surprised him. The moment he realized she wasn't opposed to…whatever happened, all joking had ceased.

The jury was still out, though. And whether they decided to take a real honeymoon or pretend that they had, people would make that assumption.

He knew he'd done the right thing by offering to marry her, but he didn't know squat about families. He'd never had a real one himself. Sure, he'd been in and out of fosters homes—some good, some not. But that wasn't the same.

Still, he'd do what he could to help Julie and the kids. But that didn't mean he wasn't nervous or stressed about how that might change his life—and not in a good way. So, for that reason, he hadn't slept worth a damn the past two nights.

Now he stood on the courthouse steps, fighting a yawn and waiting for his paper bride. When he finally spotted her heading his way, wearing a white sundress and shawl wrapped around her shoulders, his breath caught and his jaw nearly dropped to the ground.

She looked lovelier than ever. A little harried, he

supposed, and her heels tapped as she hurried up the steps to meet him.

Their marriage was based on convenience rather than love, but you'd never know that by looking at Julie. Her hair was swept into a twist, and she wore pearl earrings and a matching necklace. Had she dressed like a real bride on purpose?

"I'm sorry you had to wait," she said, her voice coming out in a nervous rush. "But there was an accident on the interstate, and it took forever to get here."

"No problem. You look great in white."

She shrugged a single shoulder. "I thought it would be appropriate."

It was. All she needed was a bouquet of flowers. Too bad he hadn't thought to purchase one for her. Of course, with the way her hands trembled, most of the petals would fall to the ground.

He brushed his lips across hers, thinking it would be a nice touch, a loving groom's expected reaction to seeing his bride. This time, it was her turn to suck in a breath.

"I…" Her eyes grew wide. "Gosh, this is so…surreal."

Yes, it definitely was. He'd expected to be nervous and fearful. Just the thought of marriage had always scared the crap out of him, but he wasn't the least bit uneasy. Probably because he was doing it for the kids.

A honeymoon, though—if that panned out— wouldn't have anything to do with the kids.

"Shall we do this?" he asked, reaching for her hand, which was clammy and trembling. He gave it a gentle squeeze, offering his support. Then they went inside.

It didn't take long for the justice of the peace, a

stoical man in his sixties, to pronounce them husband and wife. And within minutes, they held a handwritten marriage certificate that listed their names and the date.

"The legal document should be ready for you to pick up next week," the clerk said.

Adam thanked him, then led Julie out of the courthouse. Instead of talking about receptions or a honeymoon, they walked across the parking lot to the county building that housed Ms. Kincaid's office.

Once she invited them inside, Julie handed her the paperwork, the ink barely dry.

"This is only a souvenir certificate," the woman said. "It's not the legal document."

"We didn't want to wait that long to create a home for the kids," Julie said. "So we thought you'd find this, along with Jim Hoffman's email, sufficient."

The straightlaced social worker studied it carefully, her nose pinched as if she could sniff out a phony marriage without a blink. Then she blew out a sigh. "All right. But before I sign off on the paperwork, I'd like to see the house where the children will be living."

"We'll be in Julie's house," Adam said. That way, he could still take refuge at his place if family life got too much for him and the walls began to close in on him. "And we'd be happy to let you check out our living situation."

Ms. Kincaid took a look at her day planner. "How about tomorrow afternoon?"

Wow. That wouldn't give them much time to get ready for her visit.

"The later in the day, the better," Adam said. "That way, we'll be sure to be home."

Julie merely stood there, letting him do the talking. Dang, she seemed more nervous about this thing than he was. But she didn't need to be. He'd help her pull it off. As they left the office, Julie clung to his hand as if he had it all figured out and she couldn't do it without her. Little did she know that he was pedaling as fast as he could, trying to pull it all together and keep their story straight while planning for that home visitation.

She probably wasn't used to being deceitful, even when she had a good reason to be.

He'd just have to put her worries to rest once they were in the parking lot and were free to talk. Because if they had to have the house ready and the kids' bedrooms set up for Ms. Kincaid's visit, they wouldn't be going anywhere tonight except to the shopping center.

Adam would also have to go home and get a few things that would provide evidence that he was actually living in Julie's house, even if he wasn't. After that?

The jury was still out. They'd just have to wait and see what the rest of the night might bring.

Shopping was exhausting, especially when a guy hadn't slept worth a damn the past few nights, thanks to an unexpected stakeout over the weekend and his paper marriage to a beautiful blonde music therapist. But on the upside, Adam hadn't had time to consider the ramifications of a honeymoon—at least, he hadn't stressed about them.

And he certainly didn't have time to think about

any of that now, as he and Julie rushed through various stores at the Wexler shopping center, purchasing clothing and toys for the kids, not to mention room decorations, then lugging all the loot back to the cars, both of which were filling up fast.

Shopping was expensive, too. But that didn't matter when the money was spent for a good cause.

"I just thought of something else," Julie said, as they stood in yet another checkout line.

That didn't surprise Adam. Each purchase they made seemed to lead to another. "What did you forget?"

"There's a double bed in the guest room I'm converting for the kids, but Ms. Kincaid will probably insist that the kids each need to have their own."

She was probably right about that. "I guess that means our next stop is a furniture store."

"Yes, but what if they can't deliver the beds before Ms. Kincaid arrives?"

"Just show her the receipt."

Julie's brow creased. "A reasonable woman might accept something like that, but I don't want to take any chances with her."

Adam didn't blame Julie for being worried. They'd come too far to get turned down. But he didn't like seeing her stressed. So he reached out and cupped her jaw, his gaze locking on hers. "Don't give it another thought. I'll figure out something."

As she leaned her cheek into his hand, taking what little comfort he'd offered, he realized he could do better than that.

In spite of standing in the checkout line of a busy department store, he slipped his arms around her. As she rested her head against his shoulder, he savored the scent of her citrus shampoo and the way her body molded to his. A grin tugged at his lips. Shopping was also fun, not to mention arousing.

"I'll try not to worry, but…" Julie took a deep breath, then let it out slowly. "Ms. Kincaid probably expects the kids to have their own rooms. The least I can do is provide them with separate beds. I'm usually pretty good at coming up with options, but I'm drawing a blank."

So was Adam, and time was running out on them. Luckily, an idea popped up. "I'll call a furniture rental place and order two twin beds to be delivered ASAP. We can purchase something permanent later."

Julie drew away from him, her smile lighting up her pretty green eyes. "That's a perfect solution." Then her brow furrowed, and her smile faded as she studied his face. "Your eyes are red. Are your allergies kicking up?"

Adam didn't need a mirror to know what she was talking about. Each time he blinked, the lids scraped over gritty, sleep-deprived eyeballs. "It's not allergies. I've been awake nearly two nights in a row."

"Maybe you'd better take a nap."

"What?" He feigned a shocked expression. "And leave you to do all the work?" He placed a finger under her chin and chuckled. "What kind of guy do you think I am?"

She laughed. "I think you're amazing."

Adam liked the sound of that coming from her lips. Sweet lips, kissable—

"Will that be all?" the cashier asked, drawing Adam back to reality and reminding him he wasn't into public displays of affection.

Fortunately, Julie returned her focus to the task at hand and reached into her purse. "Yes, that's it."

Stifling a yawn, Adam whipped out his credit card, reached over Julie's outstretched arm and handed it to the cashier. "I'll pay this time. You got the last one."

Before Julie could object, the cashier said, "That'll be a hundred and twelve dollars and forty-five cents."

Once the transaction went through, Adam grabbed the shopping bags—all three of them. "I'll take this stuff out to the car. Then I'll call the rental company and see if we can get two twin beds—and a quick delivery."

"All right. Then I'll drive over to Target and get the bedding."

Dang. Another store and another purchase?

"Just how ready are you supposed to be?" he asked.

"I'm not sure, but I'd rather overdo it than have Ms. Kincaid think I'm not ready for those kids."

Adam studied the purchases they'd already made. What else could they possibly need? They had a few toys, several outfits, underwear, socks, pajamas, a night-light…

"What about food?" he asked. "If she's gleaned any investigative skills over the years she's worked for the county, she'll check the cupboards and the fridge. So

I'll stop by the grocery store and pick up a variety of stuff the kids will like."

"Good idea. Make sure it's healthy food. No candy or sweets. Ms. Kincaid would probably freak if she thought we'd let them load up on junk."

"I suppose you're right." But that didn't mean Adam wouldn't pick up a few of his favorite snacks, even if he had to hide them from the fussy social worker in Julie's garage. "I'll meet you at your house in an hour or so."

"Sounds good."

In spite of his best efforts to hold back another yawn, it burst out, more pronounced than the last.

"Boy," Julie said. "You really are tired."

She had no idea. And it would get worse as the night wore on.

"Are you sure you don't want to go home and take a nap?" she asked.

"No, there's too much to do." And while Adam didn't make commitments to any of the women he dated, he'd made one to Julie, at least as far as helping her get custody of those kids.

Besides, standing back and allowing Eddie and Cassie to live with the Stanfords wasn't an option.

Julie's credit card had taken a big hit today, even though Adam had paid for more than half of their purchases.

She hadn't realized how costly having children could be, but she would never complain about that. Providing Eddie and Cassie with a home and creating a family for them was well worth the expense.

On top of that, she'd had fun on today's shopping spree with Adam. They'd become a team. And maybe, with time, they'd become lovers. He was proving to be a good friend, too. If things continued the way they seemed to be going, maybe their fake marriage would become real. She actually liked the thought of that, especially since the holidays were just around the corner.

Julie didn't need to close her eyes to envision the four of them gathered in the dining room, her mother's china adorning a candlelit table laden with roast turkey, cornbread stuffing, mashed potatoes and gravy.

And then there was Christmas. For the first time in what seemed like forever, she looked forward to wrapping presents, decorating a tree and hanging stockings from the mantel.

She'd no more than parked in the driveway when Adam pulled up to the curb in front of her house, the Bronco loaded down like Santa's sleigh.

"Good news," he said as he climbed from the driver's seat. "The rental company will drop off those beds before nine o'clock this evening."

"That's a relief. I'll wash the new sheets before they get here. Can you believe it? Everything is really coming together." And more surprising, they'd been able to pull it off in less than twenty-four hours.

As Adam removed several grocery bags from the Bronco, his T-shirt stretching as his bulky muscles flexed, her heart skipped to a "Zip-a-Dee-Doo-Dah" beat. The guy was kind, helpful, handsome and strong, all wrapped up in one gorgeous, masculine package...

"There's one thing we still need to do," he said as he carried the grocery bags toward the front door.

Julie couldn't imagine what that could be. "Are you sure?"

"Absolutely. I need to bring some of my stuff over here. Ms. Kincaid seemed to question our marriage certificate, so to make sure we're not trying to pull the wool over her eyes, she might want to see evidence that I'm living here. As soon as I take the groceries and the other purchases inside, I'll go home and get some clothes to put into your closet, as well as my toothbrush, shaving kit and cologne."

"Do you think she'll investigate that thoroughly?" Julie asked.

"If she's as old-fashioned and fussy as you seem to think, I wouldn't put anything past her. And since we've come this far, why take any chances?"

"You're right." Julie took her keys from her purse and opened the front door. She quickly scanned the living room, wondering what Ms. Kincaid would be looking for in here.

Her gaze landed on the fireplace mantel, where two framed photographs—one of her parents' wedding and the other of her dad in uniform—flanked a brass clock.

"I'll need to add some pictures of the kids up there, but there's no way I can do that before Ms. Kincaid arrives tomorrow." Julie let out a ragged sigh.

"Relax," Adam said. "The woman can't expect miracles, especially when she hasn't yet decided whose petition for custody she'll support."

He was right, she supposed. "I just want everything perfect."

"I know." He brushed a kiss on her brow that sent a tingle of warmth from her head to her heart. "Don't worry. Once the kids are living here, you can take loads of pictures and put them all over the house. Other than a personal touch like that, we have everything else covered."

"Let's hope Ms. Kincaid agrees." Because Julie had no idea what she'd do if that woman found her home unsuitable.

An hour later, Adam returned to Julie's place, a small but appealing yellow house with redbrick trim and a green front door. A white picket fence enclosed a simple but well-manicured yard. It suited her.

He walked up the sidewalk with a brown bag in one hand and holding a canvas carry-on and Biscuit's leash in the other. He didn't like leaving the dog home too long. Whenever he expected to be gone any length of time, he asked a neighbor to check on her. But the woman, a kind-hearted widow, left on vacation today.

Adam yawned as he reached the front porch. The sun had set long ago. If he'd thought he was tired before, he was really winding down now. But he'd never been a quitter.

He knocked on the door.

The moment Julie spotted him on the porch and blessed him with a breezy smile, his heart took a soaring leap, jump-starting his lagging energy level.

"You're back," she said.

"I told you I wouldn't take long. I hope you don't mind that I brought the dog."

"No, not at all." Julie gave Biscuit a scratch behind the ears before stepping aside to let them inside.

"Did you get anything done while I was gone?" he asked.

"I put away the groceries and I washed the new sheets. I still have a load of clothes to wash, fold and put away. But you were right. Things might be coming together, but we probably won't finish before midnight."

His red, gritty eyes and his dragging body hoped it wouldn't take that long. At the possibility that it might, his little burst of energy fizzled.

Julie stepped aside and let him into the house. "I can guess what's packed in that overnight bag, but what's in the paper sack?"

"I stopped by a liquor store on my way here and bought a bottle of champagne. I also picked up two fluted glasses."

A smile stretched across her face. "So we're celebrating?"

"Don't you think we should?" He laughed. "Besides, if we leave the empty bottle and the glasses out for Ms. Kincaid to see, it'll make a wedding night seem more believable."

"Looks like you thought of everything."

"I try. Besides, I've worked a few child welfare cases. I also know what my social workers used to look for when checking one of the homes I lived in." He nodded toward the bay window and the front yard.

"I have some shirts and pants on hangers in the car. I'll go back for them and bring them in. Hopefully, you have some room in your closet."

"I'll make room." She looked at the clock on the bureau. "It's nearly nine o'clock. The beds should arrive soon."

As if on cue, a diesel engine sounded outside, followed by a whoosh of air as the truck braked to a stop.

"That's probably the deliverymen," Julie said.

She was right. Moments later, the doorbell rang. By the time the men set up the beds in the kids' room, and Adam hung up the last of his clothing in Julie's closet, a beep sounded from the laundry room.

"Oh, good." Julie brightened. "That's the dryer. Those sheets must be done. I'll get them."

After they'd finished making the beds—and before Adam dropped in his tracks from sheer exhaustion— he removed the bottle from the refrigerator, popped the cork and filled two flutes. He returned to the living room, where Biscuit slept in front of an easy chair and Julie stood near the hearth, studying a family photo.

She turned away when he entered and smiled when she saw what he held.

"Let's take a well-deserved break and celebrate." He handed one of the glasses to Julie.

She thanked him, then took a seat on the sofa, leaving plenty of room for him. He sat next to her, close enough to catch a whiff of her lemon-blossom scent, close enough to touch. His libido stirred.

They hadn't talked about sleeping arrangements, and while he'd like nothing more than to make love with her, he'd never let his hormones rule over his head before—and he wasn't sure this was the time to start. Besides, taking a step like that with a woman like Julie might lead to him lowering his guard and allowing an emotional intimacy he never had with any woman.

Adam had always protected his independence and privacy. But for some reason he couldn't figure out, he didn't feel the need to do so with Julie.

"It was a big day," she said. "And a busy one, but I think we're ready for Ms. Kincaid's visit tomorrow. The kids' bedroom looks awesome and their new clothes are put away. Well, other than that last load in the dryer."

He lifted his flute and studied the bubbles rising to the surface before taking a sip. He'd never really cared for champagne, but it seemed especially appropriate tonight.

"We make a good team," Julie said.

They certainly did. And for the most part, the day had been fun—even shopping, which he usually hated.

Adam clinked his flute against hers in a toast. "Here's to the kids and their new home."

Before taking a sip, Julie added, "To the kids. And to *you*. I don't think Ms. Kincaid would've even considered letting them live with me if we hadn't gotten married."

Adam reached for the champagne and replenished their glasses. He'd had his fill of the bubbly already, but he hated to waste it.

"What do you think about taking the kids on an outing this weekend?" Julie asked. "That way, if Ms. Kincaid talks to them, she'll know we're providing the kids with family activities and that they'll be happy living with us."

They'd certainly be happy with Julie. But she had a point. "Okay, let's go camping on Saturday. And on Sunday, we can take them horseback riding at my buddy's ranch."

"I'm not the outdoorsy type," she said, "but I'm a good sport."

"You'd do that?" he asked. "Sleep outdoors in a tent?"

"For Eddie and Cassie? Yes."

The thought of spending a romantic evening with Julie, after the kids went to bed…sitting under a canopy of stars, was more than a little appealing. "Just so you know," she said, "I've never camped at all. I'll try to carry my own weight, but you'll have to give me some pointers."

"Wear old clothes, boots or good hiking-type shoes, and bring a sweatshirt or jacket. It gets cold at night. I'll bring the tents and the food."

She arched a brow. "What kind of food?"

Damn. She wasn't going to be a fussy eater, was she? "The plan is to fish for our dinner."

"Ooh." She scrunched her face and slowly shook her head.

"Don't you like fish?"

"Actually, I do. But I'm not big on blood and guts, so I don't want to have to clean them. And my mom used to say, 'If you don't help in the kitchen, you don't get to eat.'"

"Don't worry. I'll clean them. But if it makes you

feel better, I'll have hot dogs in case the fish aren't biting." He lobbed a playful grin her way. "You're not opposed to eating hot dogs, are you?"

"No, I can totally handle that." She chuckled. "Tell me what I can bring."

He wouldn't let her contribute anything. Not when he had a full-time job and she didn't. Besides, she wasn't used to camping, and God only knew what kind of food she'd bring—possibly something totally inappropriate to cook or eat outdoors.

"No," he said, "I got this. I'll even bring the stuff to make s'mores for dessert."

"Sounds good." Her brow creased, and a shaky smile morphed into a frown.

"What's the matter? You look doubtful, but you're going to enjoy camping."

"I don't know about that." She laughed. "I'm not the least bit athletic, but I promise to be a good sport."

"I'm sure you will. Just agreeing to camp tells me you'll make the best of it."

"So where are we going?" she asked.

"Miller's Creek. Stan used to take me there plenty of times. It'll be a little rustic, but that's what makes it fun."

Her brow furrowed again. "What do you mean by *rustic*?"

"They have public restrooms, but not shower facilities. And we'll have to cook over a campfire. But don't worry. We'll only be there one night. Besides, a little bit of dirt and perspiration never hurt anyone."

"Okay." She sucked in a breath, then blew it out. "I can do this."

"I'm sure you can."

Adam checked the time. It was a little late, but he called Jim Hoffman and told him their plan. As he'd expected, Jim thought it was a great idea.

"I'll tell the kids at breakfast tomorrow morning," Jim said.

When they ended the call, Adam decided not to call Matt about the ranch trip until morning. Matt's uncle went to bed early, and Adam didn't want to bother him tonight.

After they'd emptied the bottle, he asked, "Can you think of anything else we should do before Ms. Kincaid arrives?"

"Not much. Once that last load in the dryer is done and put away, we can turn in for the night."

"Are you inviting me to stay?"

She paused for a couple of beats, then licked her lips. "Yes, I guess I am."

"I'm glad." He offered her a smile.

Her breath caught, as if having second thoughts.

"I'll be right back. I'm going to check on the laundry." She set her glass on the coffee table, then dashed off like a skittish filly.

Chapter Seven

Last night, after folding the last load of laundry and putting it away, Julie had returned to the living room, looking forward to ending the evening with Adam. That was, until she'd found him stretched out on the sofa and fast asleep, Biscuit lying on the floor beside him.

She'd been tempted to give him a gentle nudge and lead him to her bedroom, but she hadn't. Not when she knew how tired he was and how badly he needed to sleep. So she'd brought him a spare pillow and an autumn-colored afghan her mother had made. She'd tried to carefully slip the pillow under his head without waking him, but he didn't even stir when she tucked him in and brushed a kiss over his brow.

After locking up the house, she'd taken a shower and

then gone to bed. Apparently, she'd been exhausted, too, because she didn't wake up until morning. After making the bed, she brushed her teeth and combed her hair. Then she slipped on a robe, took her cell phone from the charger and padded to the kitchen to make breakfast and brew a pot of coffee.

She got as far as the living room, where Adam lay on his side on the sofa, embracing the pillow while sound asleep. She stopped in her tracks and marveled at his sleep-tousled hair, at his gorgeous profile.

They hadn't slept together yet, as she'd hoped they might, but who knew what the day would bring. Besides, when they did make love for the first time, it would be best if they were both wide-awake and at the top of their game.

She had no idea how long she stood in the living room, admiring Adam and wishing he'd wake up on his own. But she'd better get moving. She didn't want him to catch her gaping at him like a lovesick teenager.

Biscuit, who still lay on the floor beside the sofa, yawned, then got to her feet.

"Come on," Julie whispered. "I'll let you out in the backyard."

She opened the sliding door for the dog, then closed it. She'd hardly taken a step toward the kitchen when her cell phone rang. She nearly jumped out of her skin, then quickly answered in a soft whisper. "Hello?"

"Mrs. Santiago?" Ms. Kincaid asked.

Julie glanced at the clock on the mantel. The woman was supposed to arrive in an hour. Was she going to come early? "Yes, it's me."

"I'm afraid I'll have to reschedule my visit," Ms. Kincaid said. "One of the girls on my caseload called in tears a few minutes ago. It's not an actual emergency, but that child is overly sensitive and needs reassurance."

"I understand." And she did, but it would have been nice to know last night that they had some extra time to get the house in order.

"I've got back-to-back appointments the rest of the day, but I could come Monday morning."

"Thank you. I…" Julie cleared her throat and corrected herself. "We'd all appreciate that."

After ending the call, she turned to the sofa, where Adam had once lain and now sat.

"What's going on?" he asked as he scrubbed a hand over his brow, brushing a hank of hair back in place.

"As bad luck would have it, Ms. Kincaid can't make it this morning and rescheduled for Monday."

Adam blew out a sleepy sigh. "Well, at least we're ready for her."

"That's true."

"And it's just as well," he said, "I have plans tonight that could stretch until tomorrow morning."

Julie furrowed her brow. "What are you doing?"

"Taking you out to dinner." A bright-eyed smile dimpled his cheeks. "And fixing you breakfast in bed—if you're willing."

"Oh, I'm definitely willing."

"It's not exactly the honeymoon we talked about," he added, "but it's the best I can do, under the circumstances."

"It sounds perfect to me."

"Good. I'll pick you up around six. In the meantime, I'm going to take Biscuit home. I've got some things to do around the house." He flashed her a dazzling smile and reached for his keys, his hair mussed, his clothing wrinkled.

"Don't you want to shower first?" she asked.

"No, I'll take one when I get home."

Julie smiled as she watched him call Biscuit into the house, taking time to offer the dog some affection.

Thank goodness she hadn't totally written Adam off as a flirt and a player when they first met.

He was showing real signs of being a family man—and a husband she could love with all of her heart.

The first thing Adam did when he got home was to go online and make dinner reservations at the new steakhouse in town. He was eager to see if it lived up to all the hype.

"You ready to eat?" he asked Biscuit.

Her bushy tail thumped against the floor, as if she'd understood what he'd said. And who knew? Maybe she had.

He made his way to the kitchen, where he opened a can of dog food—the kind the veterinarian had recommended—and mixed it with the dry chow. After setting the bowl on the floor, he reached into the fridge for a bottle of water.

As he chugged a long drink, quenching his thirst, he spotted the red light flashing on Stan's answering machine. He crossed the room and pushed the play button to see who'd called.

"Hi, Stan. This is Lisa. I wasn't able to attend that gala earlier this month, so I never did connect with Adam. And I'm afraid I misplaced his number. Can you let him know that I'll be in town for a week and would love to connect with him? If he'll call me and let me know when and where, I'll make it work."

She left her phone number, and Adam jotted it down on a Post-it note. But for some reason, he wasn't eager to return her call, even though he'd promised Stan he'd meet her.

Instead, he ran a boatload of errands, finally getting home just before five o'clock.

He took a shower, shaved and got dressed, opting for a sports jacket. Then he drove to Julie's house to pick her up. When he parked the Bronco at the curb, he took a moment to study the quiet neighborhood of homes built in the 1950s. It would be a good place to raise kids. And a nice place to come home to.

Whoa. He wouldn't be living here. He shook off the thought of home and hearth and headed to the door.

He figured she'd be dressed and ready since it was about ten minutes after six already. He'd been prepared to see her dressed up, but he hadn't expected her to be rocking a black cocktail dress and heels. It wasn't quite the space girl costume of their first meeting, but it was still pretty damn sexy.

"I wondered if you'd gotten lost," she said.

He was lost when it came to seeing her looking so classy and gorgeous, not to mention framed in the doorway like a piece of art. Her blond hair had been swept into an elegant twist, revealing a pair of pearl earrings. And she'd put on makeup tonight, but not a lot. Just pink lip gloss and enough mascara to make her pretty green eyes pop.

"You look great," he said.

"Thanks. So do you." He continued to study the change in her tonight. Not that she hadn't always struck him as pretty. But dressed to the nines, she had a lady-like aura that demanded she be treated as one.

Adam had never put on any fancy airs, but he was determined to be the kind of gentleman Julie deserved this evening. At least, he would give it his best shot.

"Are you ready?" he asked.

She reached for a small clutch purse resting on a table near her door. "I am if you are."

"Then let's go," he said.

After she locked her door, he placed his hand gently on her back and escorted her to the Bronco, her heels clicking on the sidewalk, the cadence a sensual beat. He couldn't help stealing more than one glance her way.

When he stopped to open the gate, he caught a whiff of her scent. Who knew a hint of lemon could be so arousing?

He did his best to rein in his libido so he could be the mannerly suitor he hoped to be. "I hope you're hungry," he said. "I heard Sebastian's has an amazing menu."

"Actually, I am," she said. "I didn't eat lunch. How about you? Are you hungry?"

"Ravenous." Unfortunately, the growing hunger he felt couldn't be sated by food.

* * *

Julie had never felt so special in her life. Adam opened the car door for her, both at her house and again when they reached Sebastian's for dinner. He'd even pulled out her chair when the maître d' escorted them to a white-linen-draped, candlelit table for two.

She'd dated several nice guys in college. She might have married Jake, until he joined the army. Not that she didn't appreciate the military. She had the highest regard for them. But her dad's violent outbursts, his depression and prescription drug abuse had taken a real toll on her. And she'd made up her mind not to risk living through something like that again by avoiding men who had dangerous jobs.

But after tonight, she might reconsider. She'd never dated anyone who had such impeccable manners. Nor someone who was so darn good looking.

Sitting across from Adam, enjoying the romantic ambiance and a meal to die for, she felt like a princess.

After the waiter served their food, Adam asked, "So how do you like working at Kidville?"

"It's been challenging at times, but it's also very rewarding. It would be nice to be on the payroll, but I'm glad I can volunteer."

"Have you found another job yet?" he asked.

"No, but I have an interview tomorrow morning. It would be a good position, but I really hope something opens up at Kidville. I've really gotten close to Karen. And I can't think of a better employer than the Hoffmans."

"After the Rocking Chair Rodeo takes place this spring, things should look up for them financially."

"That's what Jim said." Julie took a sip of wine.

"As long as you're able to make ends meet," he added, "I don't blame you for waiting for things to come together."

"Well," she said, "it's a bit of a struggle, but not too bad. The house payments are lower than I'd have to pay in rent. And I haven't had to drain the savings account yet."

She didn't mind talking about herself, but she preferred to know more about him, about his life, his plans for the future.

"You must like Kidville, too," she said. "You've been volunteering there for six months or so."

"I guess it's my way to pay it forward."

She hadn't seen that coming, and her fork paused in midair for a moment. But she quickly recovered. "You were in foster care?"

"Yeah. And I acted out, too. Just like Jesse. I had trust issues." He shrugged. "Anyway, after I met Stan, my life turned around. And I started making better choices."

"That's the Stan who was your roommate?"

He nodded. "I...uh..." His words faltered, then he cleared his throat. "I owe that man a lot. And so I try to set the same kind of example to the kids that he set for me."

"I'm impressed."

"Don't be. It's just..." He shrugged a single shoulder.

"Well, I'm not perfect. Far from it. But now I can ride in the front seat of a patrol car, instead of the back."

He might be downplaying his own participation in turning his life around, but she still found his story admirable—him, too. There was a lot to like about Adam Santiago.

"It must have been especially tough on you when Stan died," she said. "I didn't realize that he was so much more to you than a friend and a roommate."

His only response was to nod. A few moments passed before he spoke again. "It feels good to mentor a kid the way I was mentored. In fact, if all goes well, Jesse may end up in the same foster home as his brother, which was my goal for him."

"I know what you mean," she said. "I didn't expect to grow so close to Eddie and Cassie. It warms my heart to see them smile and hear them giggle, especially Cassie."

"If our plan works, they'll end up living with you."

"I hope so," Julie said. "I'd even go so far as to adopt them. But with their mother out of the picture…" She didn't see the need to finish. He knew what she meant.

"I have a friend running the DNA tests, but it takes time."

"I'll just be happy to be their foster mother," she said.

They finished the rest of their meal in silence, although Julie caught Adam studying her over the rim of his wineglass on several occasions.

"What's wrong?" she asked.

"Not a darn thing." He gave her one of his charming smiles, setting her heart on end.

She'd been wrong about him. He wasn't the perpetual bachelor she'd imagined him to be. He was guarded, but she understood why. He'd had a sad childhood, much like the children who lived at Kidville.

After Adam paid the bill, she thanked him for a great dinner.

"It was my pleasure," he said.

As he'd done before, he opened both doors for her, first the restaurant's as they exited, then the Bronco's.

"I like your car," she said. "It's a classic, right?"

"Yeah. Stan and I refurbished it one summer."

She didn't mention that she hadn't expected him to be so mechanical, to work with his hands. Or to drive a vehicle like this. She'd envisioned him driving something fast and flashy, like a shiny red Corvette.

There was a lot about Adam that amazed her. In fact, the entire evening had taken her by surprise. Not that she hadn't expected their date to be pleasant—or even enjoyable. But a couple of weeks ago, in her earlier musing, she never imagined sharing an evening like this with him. The romantic ambiance sparked a warm glow in her chest and a smile in her heart.

When they arrived back at her house, he walked her to the porch.

As they stood on the stoop, their gazes met and locked. Pheromones stirred between them. Julie suspected he was going to kiss her good-night.

Even in the soft yellow glow of the porch light, she could see him clearly. The intensity of his gaze, the hunger in his eyes, threatened to steal her breath away and melt her into a puddle if she didn't look away. So she was surprised when he asked, "Julie, can I kiss you good-night?"

This was the first time Adam had ever asked for a kiss, the only time he'd ever felt the need to. He'd always known when a woman wanted one, and there was no doubt in his mind that Julie was ready and willing tonight. But he'd started out this evening as the perfect gentleman, and that's the way he wanted to end it.

He must have played his cards right, because a slow smile dimpled her cheeks and her eyes sparkled when she said, "You just read my mind."

He slipped his arms around her waist, but he didn't pull her close or move too fast. Instead, he merely held her, savoring her lemon-blossom scent before he slowly lowered his mouth to hers.

The kiss began slowly and tenderly, but when she parted her lips, his control faded.

Damn. He hadn't meant to get carried away, but when her tongue touched his, he was toast. Every bit of his common sense, along with the suave, mannerly image he'd tried to project all evening, dissipated in the crisp night air.

How could something that started out so innocent and gentle become so hot and arousing?

He had no idea. But one thing he did know. He was hell-bent on enjoying every moment of it.

Julie was the first to pull away, her cheeks flushed. "I...uh...don't know what to say."

Neither did Adam. For a guy who'd tossed out the idea of having a real honeymoon, he found himself running scared now. What would she expect from him?

She bit down on her bottom lip, then offered him a smile. "Would you…like to come inside?"

More than anything. But if he did, he wouldn't be able to keep up the gentlemanly facade. After kissing her, he wanted more tonight. A lot more.

Even if she was willing—and he sensed she was— making love with her was going to be a real game changer, a move he really shouldn't jump into without forethought.

"I'd like to," he said, "but I really need to get home. It's pretty late, and the last few days on the job have been grueling, so I need to get some shut-eye."

That was true, of course, although memories of that kiss were bound to keep him awake for some time.

"I've had days like that," she said. "In college, during my internships and on the job when I was a waitress, so I understand. Maybe next time."

Would there even be a next time?

Should there be?

"Sure," he said.

Rather than risk another goodbye kiss that would weaken his resolve, he turned and headed to his Bronco.

As he reached the vehicle, her front door opened then shut, signaling the end of their evening. You'd think he'd be proud of himself for doing the right thing.

So why was regret tearing him in two?

* * *

After retreating into the house, Julie remained in her living room, fingering her lips, memorizing the feel of Adam's kiss.

It had happened organically, sweet and gentle at the start. But within a couple of heartbeats, it had erupted with a passion she hadn't expected, one she'd never experienced.

Adam had kissed her senseless, weakening her knees to the point she'd had to hold him tightly for fear she'd fall to the ground if she didn't.

Whether he was dressed in a Zorro costume, serving the city of Wexler as a police detective or spending time with the kids, he wasn't just a bachelor on the prowl, as she'd once thought. He was a great guy.

He was also clearly more experienced than she was, and that kiss alone had promised sex would be out of this world.

So why hadn't he wanted to come in?

Sure, he'd said he was tired, and she believed him. He'd also been a gentleman tonight. Yet something seemed...off.

Or was she just disappointed that he hadn't brought up the idea of a honeymoon?

Okay, enough of that. She was putting way too much thought into this. He'd already gone above and beyond by marrying her so she could keep the kids.

She knew how she felt about him, but he might not be that confident. Besides, it was too early in the relationship to know for sure what was happening between them. She'd just have to let things play out day by day.

When Julie arrived at Kidville on Friday afternoon, she spotted Adam's Bronco in the parking lot. As she headed toward the classroom, the sound of children's voices and happy chatter diverted her path to the playground instead.

She didn't see him at first, but after scanning the grounds, she spotted him talking to Jesse near the water fountain. Just the sight of him spiked her heart rate and set off a tingle in her veins.

"Hey, Miss Julie!" Eddie called out from the top of the slide. "You're late. Me and Cassie were worried about you."

She smiled and approached the sweet kid's perch. "That's because I had a job interview in Brighton Valley."

His eyes grew wide, and his smile faded. "But you work *here*. You can't work someplace else."

How did she explain that she had a mortgage to pay, as small as it was?

"You'll still see me here," she said. "I love playing the guitar and singing with you guys." She just wasn't sure what her schedule would look like if she got an offer from The Traveling Minstrels, a company that provided music therapists to various convalescent and veteran's hospitals, as well as to several schools in the area.

"Guess what," Eddie said. "Ms. Kincaid came to

see me and Cassie today. She said she's going to find a home for us, but we don't want to go anyplace else. We like it here. Will you please tell her to let us stay? She wouldn't listen to me, but she has to listen to another adult."

Julie didn't dare tell the children that she was already doing her best to convince Ms. Kincaid to let them live with her because, if things didn't work out, they'd be disappointed. And they'd undoubtedly been let down too many times in their lives already.

"Sure, I'll give her a call."

"You don't have to *call* her," Eddie said. "She's in the office with Mrs. Hoffman now. So you can just go right in and tell her we don't need another place to live. You're a grown-up, so she has to listen to you."

The social worker would make the final decision. And even though they'd already scheduled the home visit, that didn't mean Julie couldn't give it another shot. And an idea struck.

"All right," she said. "I'll go talk to her."

Eddie brightened, then slid down the slide, his feet kicking up sand as he ran toward the swing set.

Before heading to the office, Julie stopped long enough to tell Karen what she was doing.

"Good luck," Karen said.

Julie stole a glance at Adam, who was looking her way. If things worked out between the two of them, as she hoped they would, the kids would have more of an impact on his life, too. And she wasn't sure how he'd feel about that.

* * *

Julie's arrival at Kidville had been a little distracting. Just the sight of her made Adam's pulse spike, but he shook it off the best he could and continued his talk with Jesse.

"I heard you went to visit Billy," he told the boy. "I'm glad. I know how much you miss your little brother."

Jesse nodded. "Yeah."

"How's he doing?"

"Okay, I guess." Jesse studied his shoes for a moment, then looked up at Adam. "Billy has his own bedroom. And he has a basketball hoop in the backyard. They even have a cat named Patches. And when she purrs, if you put your hand on her, it feels like she has a little motor in her chest."

"Cool. So he's happy?"

Jesse shrugged a single shoulder. "He said he was. And his foster parents are okay."

"I'd heard they were more than just okay. They're some of the best in the system."

Jesse remained silent for a couple of beats, then he kicked at the grass. "They said I could come back and visit again tomorrow. And that I can even spend the night."

"That's nice. They probably see that you'd be a good mentor to your brother. That you'd encourage him to make good choices."

Jesse scrunched his face, then cocked his head and looked up at Adam. "Like you do with me?"

"Exactly. I think you'd be a great older brother—if you had more opportunities to see Billy."

Jesse seemed to think on that for a while, then he nodded. "Yeah, I'd tell him not to get into trouble. And I'd make sure he got his homework done."

Adam slipped his arm around Jesse's shoulders. "I'm glad to hear that. I have faith in you."

Jesse chuffed. "You're the only one who does."

"That's not true. The Hoffmans see your potential, and so does Mrs. Wright. That's why they try so hard to direct you. They want you to see yourself the way we all do. You're a bright kid. And you could make this world a better place, like I've tried to do."

Jesse glanced up at him. "You mean, I could be a cop?"

"Sure. Or a doctor. Or a scientist…"

"Me?" he asked, still clinging to the insecurities that made him rebel against life.

"Absolutely. Believe it or not, at one time, I was headed for Juvenile Hall, but a guy I met—*my* mentor—told me he'd seen that place and convinced me that I wouldn't like it there."

"Have you seen it?" Jesse asked. "Juvie, I mean."

"Yep. And I know for a fact you wouldn't want to go there." Adam gave Jesse's shoulders a warm squeeze. "I've seen you play baseball. You've got a lot of talent. If you continue to practice and do well in school, there's nothing stopping you from being an All-Star and earning an athletic scholarship to college. But that's up to you. It's your choice. And when you grow up, you could be anything you wanted to be—an astronaut, a school teacher…"

Jesse tilted his head again, the shadows of the tree

leaves dappling his face, and grinned. "I think I'd rather be a cop—like *you*."

Warmth filled Adam's chest to the brim, just as it must have done to Stan—back in the day. "That's cool. If that's what you decide, you'll be a good one."

"You really think so?"

"I *know* so. It's my job to tell the difference between the good guys and the bad guys. And you're definitely a good one."

About that time, Danny called out, "Hey, Jesse. You gonna play catch with me or not?"

"I better go," Jesse said. "I told him I'd play with him, and like you told me, a promise is a promise."

"That's right. Now, go have fun." Adam watched Jesse jog toward Danny, then he glanced at the office, where he'd seen Julie disappear a few minutes ago.

Why hadn't she stayed on the playground? What reason did she have to talk to the administrators?

Curious, Adam crossed the playground, where Eddie was swinging.

"Hey, how's it going?" he asked the boy.

"Good, I hope. But I don't know yet." Eddie stopped pumping his feet, and the swing slowed.

"What do you mean?"

Eddie looked to the office. "I won't know for sure until Miss Julie gets back. She's going to tell Ms. Kincaid that me and Cassie don't want to move in with people we don't know."

"When it comes to having someone on your side, Miss Julie is a good one."

"Yeah." Using his feet, Eddie stopped the swing's

forward movement, but he continued to sit there. "She's going to get a new job."

Adam's gut clenched, and his brow furrowed. Would she have to move or travel with that job? Had her plans to take the kids changed? And if so, what about their marriage? Would they have to follow through on their annulment, even if he wasn't sure he wanted to break things off completely?

"Where is she going to work?" he asked Eddie. "And what kind of job is it?"

"I don't know. She didn't say. But she'll still come here. Just not as often."

Adam tried to wrap his mind around the news, which was pretty much hearsay at this point.

When the office door squeaked open and Julie stepped out, he was tempted to stride right up to her and intercept her before she reached the playground, but he remained near the swings. And that was just as well. Julie was heading his way. Or rather, she was probably coming to let Eddie know how her chat with the social worker went.

The boy got off the swing and hurried to meet her. "Did you tell her, Miss Julie? What did she say?"

"She's thinking about it," Julie said.

Eddie's lip quivered, and his eyes filled with tears. "But that means she could still make us leave, and I don't want to go someplace else. What if they're not nice to me and Cassie? Why can't we stay here?"

Adam didn't blame the kid for being afraid to move in with complete strangers. Before coming to Kidville, life had been miserable for him and Cassie, and now that they'd settled in here, they felt safe.

Julie placed her hand on Eddie's shoulder. "I'm doing everything I can to convince her that you're both doing well here, and that a move isn't a good idea—unless it's with someone you already know and like."

Eddie nodded, but he didn't appear convinced.

"But I have a surprise for you," she said. "I asked Mrs. Hoffman if you could come and stay the weekend at my house, and she thought it was a wonderful idea."

The boy brightened. "And Cassie, too?"

"Of course!"

Adam laughed. "I had a little chat with Mr. Hoffman, too. And I asked if I could take you camping on Saturday. I know this awesome lake where we can fish. It would just be for one night, but it'll be fun."

"Wow." Eddie sniffled, then lifted his arm and wiped his tears with the sleeve of his shirt. "That would be way cool. I never went camping before. And Cassie hasn't, either."

Adam knew it was just a temporary fix, but he liked seeing the kid happy.

Eddie sobered. "Isn't camping for boys?"

"Nope," Adam said. "In fact, Miss Julie is going, too."

Eddie looked up at Julie. "Cool! I'm going to tell Cassie." Then he dashed off, leaving Julie and Adam alone.

"Apparently our weekend plans were a big hit," Adam said.

"Eddie isn't the only one who likes the idea. Ms.

Kincaid seemed delighted to learn we were taking the kids for the weekend. She said she'd try to drop by to see how things are going."

"Good. I've set up that visit to my buddy's ranch on Sunday. So we're going to have a busy schedule. Ms. Kincaid might not find us at home."

"She said she'd call first. Anyway, I was thinking. Why don't you join the kids and me for dinner tonight? I'm making spaghetti."

"That sounds good. And fun. The kids are going to have a blast this weekend."

Her smile dimpled her cheeks, and her eyes glistened. "Dinner tonight is going to be a slam dunk for me, but you'll have to handle the camping prep."

"No problem. I've got everything we'll need." In fact, he would also pack a bottle of wine and a corkscrew. The kids would eventually turn in for the night, and when they did, he wanted to be ready for a quiet evening by the fire.

He didn't usually bother with anything fancy on a campout, but this one was different. Julie was different. And while she might be the kind of woman who might shake up his life, for some reason, he wasn't all that worried about it now.

Chapter Eight

By the time Adam got home from work on Friday, he'd built up an appetite and was looking forward to eating a home-cooked meal. And if truth be told, he was also eager to spend the evening with Julie and the kids.

He'd no more than opened his front door, when Biscuit greeted him with a little woof and a wagging tail. He stooped to give her some attention. "I hate to admit this," he told her, "but it's kind of nice coming home to someone, even if that someone has four legs and fur."

Biscuit gave his hand a lick.

"Come on," he said. "I'll bet you're as hungry as I am."

The first thing he did, after feeding Biscuit and before taking a hot shower, was to reach into the fridge for a cold bottle of water and down it. As he did so, he noticed the blinking red light on Stan's answering machine.

By now, most of Stan's friends knew he'd died, but if one of them didn't, Adam would have to give them the news. So he pushed Play.

"Hey, Stan. This is Lisa. It's Friday morning. I'll only be in town this weekend, and I hoped Adam and I could finally hook up. Would one of you give me a call? You have my number."

Dang. He should have returned her call, but he'd forgotten. And he did have her number. He'd written it on a pale yellow Post-it note, but he'd lost interest in going out with her. At least, for the time being. Either way, he had to tell her about Stan. So he called her back.

The call rolled to voice mail, so he left a message.

"Hey, Lisa. It's Adam. Looks like we struck out again. I've got a busy weekend, but I'd really like to talk to you." Realizing he couldn't tell her about Stan over the phone, he added, "Why don't you give me a day and time that you'll be available for coffee or a drink, and then we can finally meet."

After he hung up, his gut clenched, and a cloud of uneasiness settled over him. Lisa might think he was hoping to hook up with her at last, and if so, he couldn't blame her.

What should he tell her when they finally met and she expected to date him? That he'd changed his mind? That he was no longer available?

He raked his hand through his hair. He didn't feel like going out with anyone these days—unless it was Julie. Did that make him unavailable?

And why did he find the memory of their kisses so arousing?

He'd had plenty of kisses in the past. Only trouble was, none of them had been as amazing and unforgettable as the ones he'd shared with Julie. How could a kiss be both sweet and hot, heart-stopping and blood-pumping?

To make it worse, each kiss had reached deep inside of him, touching something he couldn't put his finger on, let alone put a name to.

So far, he'd reined in his hormones before he'd done something he might regret later. Yet for some reason, that didn't seem to bother him like it might have in the past.

Before meeting Julie, Adam would have declined a down-home, family-oriented invitation to eat spaghetti with a couple of kids. But for some crazy reason, he was actually looking forward to it. Besides, as long as Cassie and Eddie were there, he and Julie wouldn't be able to jump into anything without putting some thought into it.

But that didn't mean he wasn't planning on sharing a bottle of wine with her after the kids went to sleep.

At a quarter to six, Adam parked along the curb in front of Julie's house. Before getting out, he looked in the rearview mirror at the dog who sat in the backseat wearing a red collar and a leash.

"We're here," he said.

Biscuit's tail swished against the leather seat as if she knew her friends were waiting inside the house for her. Adam hoped Julie didn't think it was rude of him to bring a dog without asking her permission first, but he figured it would be a nice surprise for Eddie and Cassie. And if he had Julie pegged right, as long as the kids were happy, she would be, too.

Just as he was about to open the driver's door, his cell phone rang. He glanced at the display. It was his buddy, Matt Grimes, the guy he and his buddies had nicknamed Duck, returning his call.

"What's up?" Matt asked.

"Your uncle told me you were in town, and I wondered if I could bring some friends out to your place and take them riding on Sunday."

"Sure. Who are the friends?"

"A brother and sister from Kidville and the woman who's hoping to be their foster parent."

"That'd be great. I'm working on promo for the Rocking Chair Rodeo, so I might take a few photos we can use."

"No problem," Adam said.

"Hey, I was just going to drive out to the Stagecoach Inn for a couple of beers. Do you have time to meet me there?"

"I wish I could. It'd be nice to catch up, but I made plans to spend the evening with the two kids."

Biscuit woofed, clearly eager to get out and play with Eddie and Cassie.

"What was that?" Matt asked.

"I'm sort of dog-sitting these days."

"You? Mr. Won't Commit? The guy who told me a pet would cramp a bachelor lifestyle?"

"Yeah, well, don't worry. I haven't gone off the deep end." At least, not yet. And not only with the dog.

"Who asked you to watch the dog?"

"No one, actually. She was a skittish stray I stumbled across, so I've been working with her." Adam glanced in the rearview mirror. "I only plan to keep her until she's ready to live with a real family."

"Adam's Pet Rescue, huh?" Matt laughed.

"Not really. But that reminds me, I have a stakeout next week that could take a few days. Would you mind keeping her for me while I'm gone?"

"If she's that timid, do you think she can handle staying on the ranch?"

"Yeah, she's coming along okay. Besides, that cattle dog of yours is getting too old to give her much trouble."

"We had to put Lulu Belle down last week," Matt said.

"I'm sorry to hear that."

"Yeah, it was a tough decision. The vet said she had cancer and was only going to get worse. So we didn't want her to suffer."

Adam glanced in the backseat at the sweet little mutt sitting on her haunches, tongue hanging out, eyes bright. He'd never been a pet person, so he'd never been able to fully understand the people who were, the ones who called animals "fur babies" and grieved when a sick or old one crossed over a rainbow bridge. But Biscuit had touched a soft spot he hadn't realized he could have for a dog. So he'd begun to see how some people could really get attached to their animals.

"Lulu Belle and your uncle were inseparable," Adam said. "So I'll bet he's taking it hard."

"Yeah, he's been pretty quiet lately. And so has the ranch. I was going to get another dog, but Uncle George says he needs time to grieve."

"I have another place I can leave her." Adam figured he could ask Julie.

"No, I think it'll be good for Uncle George to have another dog to look after for a day or two. I'll be gone next week doing some promo for the Rocking Chair Rodeo, but he'll be here."

"We can talk about it on Sunday," Adam said.

"By the way, tell me about the woman."

Adam could tell Matt anything, but he wasn't about to admit he'd gotten married, even though it was only a temporary situation.

"She's just a friend," Adam said.

Matt didn't respond for a couple of beats. "Is she attractive?"

The cowboy was a sly one. He always had a way of digging for info without coming right out and asking.

"Yes," Adam said. "But don't jump to conclusions."

Matt chuckled. "For you, that sounds serious."

Adam had revealed more than he'd wanted to, so he changed the subject. "When is the rodeo coming to town?"

"We hit a few snags so we had to postpone it until late March. But things are back on track now. We've already placed an order for posters at the printer, and once they're ready, we'll put them up at all the local hot spots. Why don't you bring your friends? I can get you guys some VIP treatment."

"I just might do that. Eddie would like meeting some real cowboys."

"You got it. Say, I have to go. My uncle wants to have grilled tri-tip tonight, so I'd better get the fire started."

After ending the call, Adam got out of the car and walked to Julie's front porch, Biscuit's leash in one hand and a bottle of merlot in the other. He rang the bell, expecting Julie to answer. But when the door swung open, Eddie and Cassie welcomed him with a smile.

When they noticed Biscuit, they let out gleeful shrieks and dropped to their knees to greet their four-legged friend, who was just as happy to see them.

A couple of beats later, Julie approached the door-way dressed casually in a pair of black yoga pants that clung to shapely legs and a feminine white T-shirt that hung to her hips. Her blond hair, glossy and curled at the ends, tumbled over her shoulders.

She glanced first at the dog, then at Adam. "Well, look who's here."

He offered her a sheepish grin. "I hope you don't mind that I brought an uninvited guest."

"Of course not." She smiled, then addressed the kids. "Why don't you guys take Biscuit outside to play in the backyard?"

"Good idea," Eddie said. "Come on, Cassie. Let's go."

As the kids led the dog toward the sliding glass door

that looked onto a small patio, Julie returned her attention to Adam, but she didn't comment.

He shrugged a single shoulder. "I knew the kids would like it if I brought the dog. But I should have asked you first, and I'm sorry I didn't. I hope you won't throw us both out."

"No, you can both stay. I like animals, especially sweet and gentle ones like Biscuit."

Adam handed her the bottle of merlot. "I thought you might like some wine with dinner."

"It'll go nicely with spaghetti." She nodded toward the kitchen. "I need to check something on the stove, and while I'm there, I'll uncork the bottle and fill two glasses. Why don't you have a seat on the sofa? It won't take long."

Adam didn't want to sit by himself, even if it was only for a moment. So while the kids took the dog outside, then slid the door shut, he followed Julie into the kitchen.

A hearty aroma of tomatoes, basil and spice grew stronger with each step he took, filling the cozy room.

Julie stood at the stove and lifted the lid off a pot of simmering sauce. She glanced over her shoulder and blessed him with a pretty smile that damn near stole the words from his mouth.

"Is something wrong?" she asked.

He must have been gaping at her like a love-struck adolescent, so he laughed it off. "No, nothing's wrong."

In fact, everything seemed to be just right. His gaze swept over her. How could a woman be dressed so casually and be so sexy at the same time? He glanced at her bare feet, the toenails polished a bright red. Had he ever found a woman more attractive, more appealing?

"I'll open the merlot," he said. "Do you have a cork-screw?"

"It's in the drawer to the left of the sink."

"And the glasses?" he asked.

"In the top shelf of the cupboard that's to the right of the fridge."

After opening the wine, pouring two glasses and handing one to Julie, Adam asked, "Is there anything I can do to help?"

"No, I've got it under control." She turned down the burner to let the sauce simmer. When she turned around, she lifted her glass. "Since the kids are outside with the dog, let's take this into the living room."

"Sounds good to me."

Adam followed her out of the kitchen and took a seat on the sofa, next to her. He'd never been at a loss for words before, but he wasn't sure what to say, how he felt. Or what to admit. Whatever was going on was both exciting and scary.

"The kids have only been here a couple of hours," Julie said, "and the house already seems…lively." Julie turned to him and smiled. "I love having them here. And I'd give anything if Ms. Kincaid would agree to let them stay."

"How can she say no?" Adam took a sip of his wine, then set it down on one of the coasters on the coffee table. "It's going to work out. I'm also prepared to give her the results of that background check on the Stan-fords."

Julie took a deep breath, then slowly let it out. "I hope you're right. If the kids were old enough to make a decision, I think they'd like to live with me." Adam placed his hand on Julie's knee and gave it a gentle squeeze. "For the record, I would have loved having a foster mom like you."

Julie turned to him, closing the space between them on the cushions, and gazed at him in an affectionate way that set his heart rate pounding. "What was your foster family like?" she asked.

Now, there was an unexpected topic. He wasn't sure if he should be relieved or uneasy. He didn't usually talk about his past. Normally, he would have curtailed the conversation—or said he'd better go outside and check on the kids. But for some reason, he decided to be honest.

"Which one?" he asked.

Her brow furrowed, and her sweet expression turned to one of sympathy. "How many foster families did you have?"

"I had two before I ended up with Stan. The first was okay. Foster dad number one was in the military, and his wife was a special education teacher. But when he got orders to relocate to a base in Germany, he took his wife with him, and I went back into the system."

"That must have been tough."

It was, but he wouldn't admit it. Instead, he shrugged off the disappointment he'd felt at being left behind. "The second family lived in Wexler, and they enrolled me in high school. The best part of that time was making the two good friends I still have. It's just too bad foster family number two didn't see it that way."

"They didn't want you to have friends?" Julie turned toward him even more, her knee touching his and sending a shot of heat through him.

All he had to do to allow more of his leg to touch hers was to lean closer. Or he could just reach out and give her knee a sensual stroke.

Instead, he remained on topic and slowly shook his head. "They didn't like those particular friends. They thought Clay Masters and Matt Grimes were too wild and fun-loving."

"Were they?"

"Back then? I'd have to admit we were. More often than not, we all ended up in trouble at school and at home."

"Bad trouble?"

Adam shrugged. "We managed to avoid going to Juvenile Hall."

"I guess that's good."

"It depends upon who you ask. Foster dad number two had high expectations for the kids living at his house, so he grounded me and banned me from hanging out with Clay and Matt."

"I take it you didn't like that."

"Nope. And at that point, being homeless seemed like a much better option than living by unfair rules, so I shoved some of my stuff into a backpack, climbed out a window and took off."

"Where'd you go?"

"I spent a couple of nights in Matt's barn, but he

lived with his uncle George. And one morning George came in and pitched a fit. So I took off. The next night, a police officer approached me in Wexler Park. It was well after curfew, but instead of clamping down on me, he drove me to an all-night diner and made sure that I had something warm and filling to eat."

"Was that Stan?" she asked.

He nodded. "Over dessert and coffee, we kind of… formed a tentative connection. He took me under his wing, and before I knew it, he became my third and last foster dad."

"Tell me about Stan," Julie said. "What kind of man was he?"

"A great one. Good looking—the tall, dark and handsome type. He was in his late forties and had always wanted a family, but he'd never been able to commit to any one woman. Then again, maybe he'd never found the right one."

That is, not until he met Darlene. And if they'd lived… Who knew what might have happened.

"You were lucky," Julie said.

"To cross paths with Stan? That's for sure. He devoted himself to me, and I latched onto him immediately. I might have been a rebel at heart, but I wasn't stupid. I realized that I finally had someone who really cared about me."

"I guess that's why you joined the police force. You wanted to follow in his footsteps."

"Yeah. Stan was a great role model." But Adam didn't just emulate Stan in his career choice. He also enjoyed the carefree, bachelor lifestyle. Like Stan, Adam didn't believe in fairy tales.

"I better check the sauce and put the pasta on to boil," Julie said. "Then I'll ask the kids to wash up for dinner."

Good idea. Adam needed to shut his trap and quit revealing crap that he'd never shared with anyone before. "I'll tell you what. I'll tell the kids it's time to come inside and wash their hands."

She blessed him with a smile that dimpled her cheeks, and a laser of heat shot through him, creating a dull ache of sexual need. He wouldn't follow through on it tonight—not with the kids here. But he sensed this was going to be a special evening anyway, one that was cozy and warm.

As he savored the warm scent of tomatoes, basil and spice, it struck him he could get used to nights like this. It would be nice to come home to a wife and kids after a hard day on the job.

Had he met his own Darlene? The one woman who might make him reconsider his anti-commitment philosophy? Had he found whatever it was that Stan had briefly found and lost all too soon?

Adam didn't dare give that crazy idea much thought. Because if he let himself ponder it too long, he'd be more than a little disappointed if things didn't work out that way.

Julie's spaghetti sauce turned out better tonight than it ever had before, and everyone seemed to like the taste.

"A guy could get used to having meals like this," Adam said. "I eat a lot of fast food when I'm on the job, and even though I can cook, I'm not always home at mealtimes."

Julie had once thought that Adam was the epitome of a die-hard bachelor, but he'd shown her another side. He was so good with the kids, and he'd practically adopted the stray dog himself, even if he hadn't admitted it yet.

Wasn't that a sign that he was open to falling in love someday and creating a family?

She didn't dare to pin her hopes on something like that, at least, not yet. But her life had changed in a good way ever since meeting him and becoming...his friend. And now she was also his wife, even if their marriage wasn't supposed to last.

After dinner, she served strawberry ice cream for dessert. Adam and the kids helped wash the dishes, then they all went to the living room, where they watched an animated movie on television.

Every once in a while, Julie stole a peek at Adam, who seemed to be enjoying the cartoon as much as the kids were.

During one especially funny part, he turned to her, lowered his voice and said, "This is hysterical. I had no idea they used so much adult humor in a cartoon made for kids."

"I think the idea is to appeal to both children and their parents. That way, Mom and Dad are more eager to take their kids and to spring for the price of admission if they think they'll enjoy it, too."

"Good point."

When the cartoon ended, Julie told the kids it was time to brush their teeth and get ready for bed.

"Are Adam and Biscuit spending the night, too?" Eddie asked.

Julie's cheeks warmed, and she knew better than to look at Adam, who answered for both of them.

"No," he said, "Biscuit and I will be going home soon. But don't worry. We'll have fun again. My friend has a ranch, and earlier today, I asked him if I could take you guys horseback riding on Sunday."

"That would be way cool!" Eddie turned to his sister, who was nodding enthusiastically, then back to Adam. "Do we need cowboy boots? If so, we don't have any."

"Not this time." As Julie took the kids to help them get ready for bed, Adam remained behind and said, "There's some wine left. Do you want to finish it off?"

She also had a full bottle in the pantry that had been there since her next-door neighbor brought it over as a Christmas gift. But she needed to keep her wits about her, especially with the kids here tonight. "How about a cup of decaf?" she asked. "I can make a pot after the kids go to sleep."

"I'll make it."

"You'll find a new can, as well as the filters, in the cupboard above the coffee maker."

"How do you take yours?" he asked.

"Cream and sweetener. You'll find half-and-half in the fridge and sugar in one of the canisters on the counter."

"Leave it to me."

By the time the kids had washed up, brushed their teeth, put on their pajamas and climbed into bed, Julie caught the aroma of a fresh brew emanating from the kitchen. After tucking them in and giving them a good-night kiss on the brow, she returned to the living room, where Adam had a cup of decaf waiting for her.

She took it, then settled in on the sofa. She'd planned to keep a safe distance this time, but ended up sitting close enough to reach out and touch him.

"What will you do with the dog while you're gone next weekend?"

"I've got it covered. I've asked Duck to watch her while I'm gone."

"Duck?" Julie laughed. "Don't tell me you found a stray mallard and took it in, too."

"I'm sorry." Adam's smile dimpled his cheeks, making him look boyish and sweet. "That's what I call Matt Grimes, my old high school buddy. We all had nicknames back then, and every now and then they creep back into our conversations."

Julie lifted her cup. She hadn't tasted it yet, but by the creamy color, she saw that Adam had doctored it up, just the way she liked it. She blew across the brim to speed up the cooling process so she could take a sip. "It's nice that you're still connected to your friends from high school."

"Yeah, that's true. But we don't get to see each other as often as we once did."

She took a drink. *Mmm. Perfect.* "Why don't you guys get together as much?"

"Matt still officially lives on the Double G, a ranch in Brighton Valley, but he's a champion bull rider, so he's out of town a lot."

"How did a real live cowboy end up with a nickname like Duck?" she asked.

"Back in the day, the high school girls used to flock around him. A couple of them told him he had a sexy cowboy swagger. After that, he strutted around like a peacock all day. So we told him he waddled like a duck, and the name stuck."

"I take it he really didn't waddle," Julie said, savoring another taste of coffee.

"Heck no. But Bullet and I didn't want the girls' comment to go to his head. For the record, Duck was cowboy through and through—and he still is. No doubt women still tell him he has a sexy swagger."

"You and *Bullet*, huh?"

"That would be Clay Masters. He was a star quarterback with a dead aim."

"So he threw the ball like a bullet?"

"Yes!" Adam tossed her a wink. "You're catching on."

She was also learning a little more about the guy she'd sized up at first sight, only to learn she'd been wrong. And that realization made her want to know even more about him—his past, his day-to-day life, his plans for the future.

"So why did they call you Pancho? Your name is Adam. I had a friend in third grade, and that's the nickname his parents called him. Is your *middle* name Francisco?"

"No, not even close. I'll tell you how that came about. Back in the day, I was the wildest and biggest rebel of the group. A real teenage badass. So one day, after a lecture in US history class, they dubbed me Pancho Villa. Pancho for short."

"Okay, I get it." She also saw the transformation he'd made, thanks in large part to Stan. "So the rebellious teenage boy made a U-turn and became a law-abiding cop?"

"That's about how it all went down." He lifted his mug and took a drink.

She did the same, noting again that hers seemed to taste better than usual this evening.

They sat quietly for a while, each lost in their thoughts, or so it seemed. Every once in a while, she stole a glance at Adam, then quickly took a drink of her coffee. As the clock ticked softly on the fireplace mantel, she'd never felt so…cozy. So comfortable.

It was nice being with Adam, especially now that the kids were asleep. He was a real live hero who kept the city of Wexler safe, and he was becoming her personal hero, too. A man she could look up to, depend upon. A husband she could easily fall in love with—if she hadn't done so already.

Every time the handsome hunk tossed her a charming smile, it turned her inside out. He was also a darn good kisser, which probably meant he'd be an amazing lover.

Had his thoughts drifted that way? Was he thinking about kissing her again?

"It's been a nice evening," he said.

"I think so."

He took in a deep breath, then let it out. "I probably ought to go."

"Do you have to?" Her cheeks warmed. It sounded as if she was inviting him to spend the night. And she would, if the kids weren't here. She didn't want any slip-ups before Ms. Kincaid made her decision. "I mean, do you have to go now?"

"I should. Otherwise, I might forget the kids are in the house. And I'd hate to have them wake up and find us kissing...or whatever."

If she was allowed to keep the kids, they'd have to get used to seeing her and Adam kiss. She'd also have to put a lock on her bedroom door, just in case.

"I'd hate for them to mention anything to their social worker," Adam added. "You don't need any bad press."

"That's true. But just for the record, if things weren't still hanging in the balance, I'd invite you to spend the night."

"And I'd stay in a heartbeat."

Their gazes locked for a moment, then he pulled her into his arms and drew her mouth to his. This time, the kiss exploded with passion, and as they stroked and caressed each other, she yearned for him even more.

Adam slipped his hand inside her blouse, his fingers scorching her skin, taunting her, tempting her to throw caution—and Ms. Kincaid—to the wind.

When he reached her breast, his thumb skimmed over her nipple, sending her senses reeling. As he worked his magic, an ache settled low in her core.

He was good at this, she thought. So good.

But they had the kids to think about. And even if she had a lock on the bedroom door, which she didn't now, making love with him tonight didn't seem right.

Reluctantly, she pulled her lips from his. "I'm sorry. If I don't stop things now, I might not be able to later."

"What can I say?" A slow smile lit his eyes. "I told you I had a rebellious streak."

Maybe he did, once upon a time, but Julie doubted he still had one. She smiled, glad they could make light of something so… Well, so tempting, so arousing.

Adam got to his feet. "I'll pick you and the kids up tomorrow morning around ten o'clock."

"All right." She straightened her blouse, wishing she could remove it instead. "I saw Biscuit sleeping on the bedroom floor, keeping watch over the kids."

"I'd leave her here, but I didn't bring her food." He retrieved the leash from the lamp table, where he'd left it when he arrived.

When he returned to the living room with Biscuit, he said, "When the time is right, we can finish what we started tonight. And believe me, it'll be worth the wait."

She didn't doubt that for a minute. She just wished they didn't have to wait too long.

Chapter Nine

Julie might not have any experience with camping, but that didn't mean she wasn't smart enough to do an internet search and learn all she could. It might only be a one-night trip, but at least Adam wouldn't think she was a total novice and completely out of her element.

So on Saturday morning, when Adam arrived at her house to pick up her and the kids, she was not only dressed and ready to go, she was standing on the front porch. Beside her sat a bulging backpack that carried everything she could possibly need—sunblock, insect repellent, anti-bacterial wipes, paper towels, two large jugs of water, some healthy snacks, a couple of plastic trash bags, a change of clothes and a toiletry bag. Hopefully she hadn't forgotten anything.

"Good morning," Adam said as he climbed out of

the driver's seat wearing hiking boots, worn Levi's, a flannel shirt and a dazzling smile that set her heart on end. "I'm glad you're ready. And by the way, you've got on the perfect outfit for camping."

She glanced down at the old pair of Skechers she wore, as well as the worn jeans and faded sweatshirt. Then she looked back at him, watching him make his way toward her. "I knew better than to put on anything new. I figured I'm bound to get dirty before we're done." She'd also pulled her hair into a messy ponytail, assuming she'd be hard-pressed to keep it brushed and neat.

Adam met her on the porch and reached for her backpack, but before heading back to the car, he paused and swept a gaze over her. An appreciative glimmer lit his eyes. "You look great."

Pride rose up in her chest. She might be dressed in ratty clothes, but she'd taken the time to apply a little makeup—waterproof mascara and a cherry lip gloss. "Thanks. So do you."

And did he ever. His dark hair glistened in the morning sun. His eyes, the shade of warm honey, sparkled. A smile dimpled his cheeks…

She fought her attraction by calling the kids from inside, where they'd been having a morning snack at the kitchen table.

"We're coming!" Eddie called out, as he and his sister dashed out of the house and hurried to the car, where Biscuit sat in the back.

After locking the door, Julie carried her gym bag to the car and handed it to Adam.

"Are dogs allowed at the campsite?" she asked, as Adam tried to cram her bag, as well as both backpacks, in the rear of the vehicle, which was already full.

"If they're on leashes. I could have left Biscuit at home and asked my neighbor to look after her, which is what I usually do when I know I'm going to be away from the house for a long period of time. But I thought bringing her along would be a nice treat for the kids."

Adam clearly loved that sweet dog. Julie chalked that up as one more reason to believe that she'd completely misread him on day one.

She glanced at the top of his Bronco, where he'd secured a couple of long boxes with green bungee cords on the roof rack. "Are you sure we're only staying one night? It looks as though you expect to be roughing it for a week or more."

"Yep. I've brought two tents, sleeping bags, a first aid kit, wood for the fire and food." He opened the passenger door for her, and as she took a seat, she caught a hint of aftershave, a woodsy scent that confirmed he was an outdoorsman at heart.

About thirty minutes later, as the Bronco kicked up dust and bounced along a rutted dirt road that led to Miller's Creek, Julie said, "Boy, you weren't kidding when you said this place was 'rustic.' It's rugged, too."

"That's what I like about it."

For a guy who'd refurbished a classic vehicle and kept it shiny and clean, he didn't appear to be concerned about the bumps or dust.

Adam steered the vehicle to the left and drove under an archway of weathered wood, its lettering, once painted black, no longer legible. "As far as I'm concerned, this place is Wexler's best-kept secret."

"It's certainly pretty out here." Julie studied the setting—a pristine lake that wasn't much bigger than a pond, dogwood trees that rustled in the wind. She might not be a camping enthusiast, but if she had to spend a rustic night outdoors, this would be a nice place to do it.

She counted ten different campsites, only two of which were occupied—one by an older couple in a small motor home with a faded blue awning and the other by a couple of teenage boys with a green pup tent. She also spotted a small cinder block building that had to house the restrooms.

Adam drove to the campsite farthest from the others and parked. Then he turned to the backseat and asked the kids, "What do you guys think?"

Eddie, who'd been studying the area wide-eyed, turned to his sister. "This is awesome, huh, Cassie? It's going to be way cool."

The little girl nodded sagely. Even the dog, whose tongue hung out of its mouth as it panted, appeared to agree.

"When are we going to put up the tents?" Eddie asked.

"Right now. But first, someone is going to have to take Biscuit for a walk."

Cassie tugged at Adam's sleeve. "I… I'll…do it."

He smiled and placed his hand along the side of her head, stroking the blond strands. "That would be great.

Thank you, honey." Then he turned to Julie. "Would you mind tagging along with them?"

"Not at all." Julie glanced at the rack on the roof of the Bronco, assuming several of the long boxes held the tents. "You have a lot of stuff to unpack. Do you want us to help you unload the car first?"

"No, that's not necessary." Adam placed his hand on the boy's small shoulder. "Half the fun is in setting up camp. It'll also give Eddie and me a chance for guy-talk."

"Then thank you for letting us off the hook," Julie said. "We'd rather enjoy the pretty surroundings anyway."

"Good choice." Adam lifted the Bronco's back hatch, then lowered the tailgate. The vehicle was jam-packed with gear, including an ice chest and what appeared to be a box of food.

Again, Julie hesitated. "Are you sure we can't help?"

"Yep." Adam turned to Eddie and winked. "We've got this, don't we?"

Eddie nodded firmly, seriousness stamped across his face.

Julie fought a smile, yet she was reluctant to leave. For one reason, she always tried to pull her own weight. She'd also enjoy watching Adam's muscles flex as he lifted boxes.

Then again, taking Biscuit for a walk would allow her time to talk to Cassie. And if she was lucky, she might entice the girl to open up and speak more than a few words at a time.

"All right then." Julie took the dog's leash, then

reached for Cassie's hand. "Come on, sweetie. Let's check out our surroundings."

They took their time walking along the creek, taking in the sounds of running water, twigs breaking under their feet and the caws of a territorial black crow.

As Julie took in a deep breath, savoring the fresh air and the warmth of the sun on her face, Cassie gasped, then pointed ahead. "Look."

Julie froze in her tracks, fearing a snake or a lizard or…maybe even a bear. "What is it?"

"A pretty rock." Cassie released Julie's hand and hurried toward a small reddish stone. She lifted it off the ground, studied it in awe then turned to Julie with a smile.

"You're right," Julie said. "That is a pretty one. And it's shaped like a heart."

"I know!" The child studied her precious find.

"Let's take it back to camp with us. Maybe you can collect more things to help you remember what we did today."

Fifteen minutes later, with their pockets stuffed with more rocks for their collection, Julie and Cassie returned to the campsite, where Adam had already set up two small tents, one for her and Cassie to share, the other for him and Eddie.

"It's looking good," Julie said, although she couldn't help admiring the dark-haired hunk who was lifting the last box from the roof rack, his muscles flexing, the breeze ruffling his dark hair. He was strong, confident and handsome. He'd make the perfect husband. Not just on paper, but in every sense of the word.

After placing the box of food on the wooden picnic table, next to a couple of fishing poles and several battery-operated lanterns, Adam handed a sleeping bag to Eddie. "Here you go. Let's put two of these in each tent."

Next Adam passed another sleeping bag to Cassie. "Help your brother set these out. Okay?"

The girl nodded eagerly, then hurried to do as she was told. Julie walked over to the picnic table and studied the contents of the box. Then she peeked into the ice chest. In addition to hot dogs, ketchup, small boxes of juice and milk, Adam had packed a bottle of white wine.

Her cheeks warmed, and a smile stole across her face. The day had started out great, and the night promised to be even better.

When the kids returned from setting out the sleeping bags, she did her best to rope in her stray thoughts and to mask the grin that kept popping up whenever she thought about the sun going down and the moon rising.

"I love it out here." Eddie gave his little sister a nudge. "Don't you, Cassie?"

She nodded but didn't say a word this time. But that was okay. She'd not only been talking more, lately, but she was also stronger, braver and happier than when she first arrived at Kidville.

And that was just one more reason for the social worker to let both Eddie and Cassie either live with Julie or to remain at Kidville.

"What's the big trash bag for?" Eddie asked Adam.

"We need to clean up after ourselves. We don't want to leave a mess."

Responsible. Hardworking. A guy who cared about kids. Adam Santiago had proven to be the kind of man Julie had always dreamed of finding. And the fact that he was also drop-dead gorgeous was an extra perk.

For a camping novice, she looked forward to a new adventure, to watching the sun set and, when darkness fell, sitting around a campfire. As much as she enjoyed being with Eddie and Cassie, she was also looking forward to the time they went to bed, when she'd be able to spend the rest of the evening with Adam.

"So how did you like fishing?" Adam asked Eddie as they headed back to camp.

"It was sort of fun, but we didn't catch any fish to eat for dinner."

"Maybe next time they'll be biting and we'll catch a bunch. But don't worry about going hungry. We're going to fill up on hot dogs."

"But how?" the boy asked. "I didn't see any pots or pans."

"Don't worry. I've got it covered. I brought metal coat hangers."

The boy scrunched his face, clearly confused. "Huh?"

Adam chuckled. "We'll untwist the hangers, stick a hot dog on the end and roast them over the campfire. Just wait and see. It'll be even more fun than fishing."

Sure enough, after Adam got a good fire going in the pit and untwisted four coat hangers, he showed the kids and Julie how to stick the end through the wiener and hold them over the flames.

"Hey," Eddie said. "This *is* fun! And holding on to this wire is kind of like a fishing pole. But instead of a fish at the end, I got a hot dog."

Adam shot a glance at Julie, who was seated next to Cassie. Her blond hair had been pulled back in a pony-tail, and her cheeks were flushed, her eyes bright. She projected a girl-next-door image. But instead of avoiding her, like he'd first considered doing, he wanted to scoot closer, to sit beside her, to watch the flickering flames as the fire died down and to count the stars.

Sheesh. Could he get any cornier than that?

Adam glanced at Biscuit, who sat beside him, watching them all like a family pet, her tail swishing against the ground. He removed an uncooked beef frank from the package, broke it in two, then offered her a bite. She sniffed at it, then drew back. She repeated that same movement before giving in and taking the meat she clearly wanted. Then she gobbled it up.

She'd come a long way. And so had Eddie and Cassie, who smiled and giggled and chattered like other kids, the ones who grew up in decent homes with loving parents. Thinking about their metamorphosis and knowing he'd played a part in it brought a smile to his face and filled his chest with warmth.

After they'd eaten their hot dogs, Adam showed them how to make s'mores for dessert.

"I could live out here forever," Eddie said as he licked his sticky fingers.

"Me, too." Cassie looked up at the night sky, at the

twinkling stars overhead, then broke into a bright-eyed grin. "This is my funnest day ever."

"It sure is special." Julie looked at Adam and blessed him with a smile, making him feel pretty damned special, too.

After helping the kids wash their gooey hands and faces, Julie said, "Next time I'll have to bring my guitar."

Eddie pointed to the Bronco. "But then we'd have to bring two cars because I don't think we could fit another thing or person or dog in that one."

"Good point," Adam said.

"I like it when you play music," Cassie said.

"Me, too." Eddie reached out to the dog and stroked her head. As the critter leaned into his hand, the boy took the hint and scratched behind her ear.

"We don't need an instrument to sing," Julie said. "I'll show you."

She broke into their favorite song she'd taught them, about a little speckled frog, and even Adam joined in. Then she taught them more silly ditties, about a peanut on a railroad track and an old woman who swallowed a fly.

Adam found himself enjoying the night in a way he hadn't expected to. And while this evening was a far cry from the many camping trips he'd taken with Stan at this very same campsite, it was turning into a special memory of its own.

Before long, the kids began to yawn. So Julie took them to the restroom, their way lit by the light outside the cinder block building. When they returned to camp,

Julie told the kids to put on their pajamas. Then she tucked them in, one at a time, and promised that she and Adam would join them shortly.

He probably should have helped with the bedtime stuff, but he felt out of his league, so he took the dog for a walk instead. Besides, the maternal role seemed to come naturally to Julie. Not that he had any first-hand experience to go by himself, but the kids sure responded to her TLC.

Finally, when he returned, he found Julie sitting by the campfire, and he placed his chair next to hers.

When it came to romance, Adam didn't need any props, but this was different. Julie was different.

He walked over to the icebox and pulled out the bottle of chardonnay he'd packed. "How about a glass of wine? I wasn't sure how things would go today, and I thought we might want to unwind at the end of it."

"I'm feeling pretty mellow," she said, "but a glass of wine sounds good."

"We'll have to drink out of disposable cups."

"That's fine with me. I expected us to be roughing it tonight."

Adam filled two red plastic cups, then handed one to Julie and took his seat beside her. When she broke into a bright-eyed smile, the sheer pleasure and force of it knocked him off stride, and he couldn't remember why he'd once thought they weren't well suited. In fact, he seemed to have forgotten just about everything but his name.

Up until now, he'd regretted that kiss they'd shared. Not because it hadn't been hot, but because it had. And tonight, while crickets chirped in the background and the flames licked the logs in the fire ring, it seemed like the perfect time for another one.

The old Adam, the one Julie didn't know, wouldn't have given it a second thought. He would have known just what to do. But this new guy, the one he was trying to be, wasn't so sure of himself these days.

Julie set aside her wine and went to check on the kids, who'd been quiet for about fifteen minutes. And just as she'd expected, they had both crashed, even with the battery-operated lanterns casting a soft white light inside.

When she returned to the firepit and headed for the lawn chair she'd just vacated, Adam asked, "Are they asleep?"

"Yes, and I don't think it took very long, either." She sat in the chair next to his, which seemed a wee bit closer to his than it had been before, but probably wasn't. Maybe knowing that they were on their own now made it seem that way. Either way, she didn't mind. She'd been looking forward to having some quiet time with him.

"They had to be exhausted," she added.

"They definitely had a good time today."

"That's for sure." Julie glanced at Biscuit, who was curled up next to the fire. The poor dog was worn out, too. But Julie wasn't the least bit sleepy.

She took a sip of wine from the plastic cup. "I can see why you like camping, especially here. It's so peaceful."

"I know. And when you're an unhappy kid with a king-size chip on his shoulder, it can be healing."

She turned, her knee brushing up against his thigh. Warmth that had nothing to do with the campfire radiated through her. She felt compelled to dwell on it, to enjoy the way it stirred her hormones, but there was so much about Adam she wanted to know, and he'd just broached the subject of his past again.

"Your early years must have been pretty rough," she said.

"To say the least. I grew up in a broken home, which would have been bad enough. But the dynamics kept changing."

"How so?"

"Let's just say my mom never slept with a man she didn't marry. And the men seemed to come in and out of our lives like they were passing through a revolving door."

Julie's life had been blessed by comparison, although hard times came after her father returned from the war. "I take it your dad was out of the picture."

"Completely. I never knew him. He left when I was a toddler. When I was four, she married a functional alcoholic who put food on the table and kept a roof over our heads. But once he got home each night, he opened a case of beer, parked in front of the TV and drank until he fell asleep."

That probably meant Adam hadn't had to deal with violent outbursts like she had. At least, that was her take on it.

"Mom's second marriage might have lasted if the

guy hadn't decided to change his routine one evening. On his way home, he stopped by a local bar. Several hours and about seven drinks later, he died in a single-car accident, his blood-alcohol level two times the legal limit."

Julie winced. "That's too bad."

"In a way, it was. But he had an insurance policy that paid off the mortgage and left my mom with a small nest egg."

"I guess there's always a bright side."

Adam chuffed. "That might have been a lifesaver, if she hadn't remarried. My second stepdad was a charmer with a gambling addiction. When his luck ran out, so did he, leaving my mom in a real financial bind. Come to find out, she'd refinanced her house and depleted her savings account, as small as it was, to pay off several of his gambling debts. After they divorced, she had to get two jobs to make ends meet. And that left me to fend for myself as a latchkey kid."

"No wonder you have a soft spot for children."

"Yeah." Adam studied the flames, which were dying down. A couple of logs sat next to the firepit, but he didn't move. "If my mom had remained single, we both would have been better off, but the third guy also had a drinking problem. And when he drank, he got mean. Instead of shutting down in front of the TV for the night, he'd get mad as hell for no reason and smack anyone who got within his reach."

She'd been wrong. He'd suffered violence in his life, too. "I'm sorry."

He tore his gaze away from the fire. "Hey, it happens. There are a lot of kids who have it worse than I did. At least the neighbors finally called the police, and child protective services stepped in and placed me in foster care."

She hurt for the little boy he'd once been, yet she was proud of the man he'd become in spite of it all.

"That's enough about me," Adam said. "You had a charmed childhood, and I don't want to bore you with any more of the ugly details of mine."

"I'm not the least bit bored. And for the record, my early years were wonderful, but my life took a bad turn after my mom passed away."

"How did she die?"

"She had an aggressive form of pancreatic cancer and died within a month of the diagnosis." Julie glanced up at the sky, as if her mom was looking down on her and offering compassion for the pain Julie had felt at losing her, at the fear she'd felt facing an unknown future without her mother.

"How old were you?" Adam asked.

"Fifteen. The army sent my dad home in time for the funeral, but I barely recognized him. He was gaunt, pale and had a dazed look in his eyes I assumed was caused by grief. And some of it probably was. I didn't know it then, but he was suffering from PTSD."

She wasn't sure why she was opening up and sharing her personal pain. But it only seemed fair, since he'd opened up to her. So the words and memories seemed to flow. "My dad used to have these loud, violent outbursts. I did my best to keep things peaceful at home. I was afraid the neighbors would complain, that if they called the police, they might lock him up and send me into foster care."

"That must have been tough on you," Adam said.

"It was, but I noticed that when I played the guitar and sang, he'd settle down."

"Is that what led you to become a music therapist?"

"Yes. It's a good fit, I guess." She blew out a soft sigh. "I'm glad I was able to give my dad a respite from his nightmares, but his peace didn't last too long after I strummed the last chord."

"Did your dad eventually get professional help?" Adam asked. "TVA has programs that are pretty effective."

"I begged him to talk to someone, but he told me he was okay. He'd work it out himself. But one day, during my first year in college, the haunting memories got to be too much for him, and he decided life wasn't worth living anymore. I came home one afternoon to find him dead from an overdose. He left a note, apologizing for being a loser and a burden."

"I'm sorry," Adam said.

"Me, too. It seemed so unfair. To him, to me… But I did my best to move on. He left the house to me, so it's mine now. And so is the mortgage. But that's okay. The payment is pretty small. And I still have a savings account to help out until I start working full-time."

Adam reached out and took her hand in his, which both surprised and pleased her. She couldn't remember when she'd last felt someone's support, and it was nice to have his. But it was more than friendship that was heating her skin, more than his encouragement rising up inside.

"Everything will work out." Adam gave her hand a gentle squeeze, his grip insisting his words were true and suggesting that he'd continue to see her through whatever lay ahead.

She hoped she wasn't reading too much into his kindness, but when she turned to him and caught him gazing at her with an intensity that warmed her from the inside out, she somehow knew his claim was true. It would work out—the mortgage, a full-time job, the future.

As he leaned in for a kiss, her lips parted. Their mouths met with conviction, with purpose. And she lost herself in his arms. That might have frightened her before, when she'd thought that Adam was a player. But she'd fallen in love with the man she'd once told herself was the last guy in the world she ought to date.

And boy, was she glad she'd been wrong.

Adam kissed Julie softly at first, respectfully. But the moment her lips parted, his tongue swept into her mouth, and he was toast.

Heat shot through his veins, lighting a blaze in him as if she'd tossed lighter fluid on the dying embers in the campfire.

A kiss like this wasn't meant to be shared while sitting awkwardly in foldable outdoor chairs, but it didn't seem to matter if they tipped over and landed in the dirt. All he knew was that he couldn't seem to hold Julie close enough or kiss her deep enough.

She tasted like roasted marshmallows and melted chocolate, a lingering remnant of the sweet, sticky dessert they'd shared. He'd thought he'd had his fill of the gooey things, but right now, he hungered for *s'more*. S'more of this. And definitely s'more of her.

He stroked the slope of her back, but his hands wadded up in the baggy sweatshirt material, hampering his exploration. He was tempted to reach under the fabric and seek her skin. If he did, would she object?

Her hands were doing a little exploration of their own, so she'd probably welcome it.

The dog whimpered, drawing him back to reality. He hoped the kids were good sleepers. If they woke up now, the timing would suck. He'd better slow things down.

But tell that to his libido. Dammit. He couldn't seem to keep his lips or his hands to himself.

The dog's whimper became a soft whine. Was it jealous of the attention he was giving Julie?

Maybe Biscuit was bothered by the attention she was giving to him, because she was kissing him back as if they were seasoned lovers who knew all the right sexual buttons to push.

The dog whined once more, and Julie ended the kiss before Adam had a chance to.

"Oops." She straightened in her seat and looked at the doe-eyed critter who sat at their feet, its tail swishing in the dirt. "I guess Biscuit thinks we're ignoring her."

Maybe so, but Julie had Adam's full attention right now, and he didn't have any left to share with the dog.

Where did the woman learn to kiss like that?

She turned back and gazed at him, her cheeks flushed, her lips plump from his recent assault, and smiled shyly. "Biscuit has grown pretty attached to you."

Maybe. But Adam didn't get attached to animals. Or to women.

At least, he never had before. But the raging firestorm Julie had set off in him hadn't shown any sign of chilling in the night air. The physical arousal he could deal with. But the emotional stuff?

A moment of panic kicked in, but he did his best to tamp it down.

"You know," she said, flashing him a pretty smile, "I'm going to like being married to you."

"Me, too. At least, as long as it lasts."

She stiffened, as if he'd said the wrong thing.

But had he? He'd already become the proud owner of a fur baby. Was he up for anything long term, especially a real marriage?

"I…uh…" Oh, man. He'd never been speechless at times like this. He couldn't afford to be. He'd always made it a point to make sure there were no misunderstandings with women. That's why he'd suggested an annulment after Julie had custody of the kids.

Had she forgotten?

She bit down on her lip. Then she glanced first at one tent, then at the other. "I don't drink alcohol very often. And that wine really hit me hard." She gave a silly little shrug and laughed it off. "I'd better turn in for the night. The Hoffmans expect us to watch over Eddie and Cassie. They might be out for the count, but I shouldn't be."

"You're right." Adam raked a hand through his hair, as if a movement that simple might put things to right.

Julie stood and stretched. Then she yawned. Whether

it was real or fake, he couldn't tell. "I'll see you in the morning."

"You don't have to—"

"Oh, yes, I do. I need to turn in before my legs give out on me." She nodded toward the tent where Cassie slept. "I'll see you in the morning."

"Good night." Adam watched as she opened the canvas door flap and crawled inside, but she didn't turn on the lantern. Had she collapsed in a drunken heap?

It didn't seem likely.

Maybe he ought to check on her, but if he did, she might want to talk things out. And there was no way he'd do that when his thoughts were so tangled that they'd probably trip him up before he took a single step.

Biscuit placed her chin on his knee, as if she sensed his distress and wanted to offer her support. He caressed her head while he studied Julie's tent.

He should try to come up with something to explain his awkward reaction, but the only one he had was that his feelings for her scared the crap out of him. And the thought of losing his independence damn near paralyzed him. So he remained right where he was, seated by a fire that had nearly died out, watching the smoke drift away.

And wondering what in the hell he was going to do about Julie.

Chapter Ten

By the time Julie escaped to the privacy of her tent, her cheeks burned with embarrassment, her chest ached with disappointment and her eyes stung with unshed tears. The light from the community bathroom, which was located several campsites away, provided a faint yellow glow through the open flap of the netted tent window, but hardly enough to see.

She would have turned on the battery-operated lantern, but she wasn't about to provide Adam with a show, even if it was only a silhouette. Not that it mattered if he watched her shadowed image get ready for bed. She just didn't want him to see her wipe away her tears. So, taking care not to wake Cassie, she fumbled in the semi-darkness to slip off her shoes, remove her jeans and put on the flannel pajama bottoms she'd had in her backpack.

By the time she climbed inside her sleeping bag, tears trickled down her cheeks, and the ache in her chest was as strong as ever. She wanted to blame Adam for her disappointment, but it was her own fault for ignoring her instincts and pinning her heart on the mythical idea that something special had happened between them.

She let out a soft sigh, the only sound she dared to make, and lay in the dark for the longest time. She tried her darnedest to think about anything other than Adam and that last kiss, but in spite of conjuring up a happy childhood memory, she kept going back to the blasted kiss.

As far as she was concerned, each one she'd shared with him had been amazing, earth-shattering and even more arousing than the last. And while she'd known this wasn't the time or place for making love, she'd hoped it would happen eventually—and sooner rather than later.

She'd actually thought that their marriage would eventually become real. In her naïveté, she'd thought that things between them had been moving along nicely, like two singers harmonizing a cappella. But she'd been wrong. The minute he'd reminded her that their relationship was only temporary, he'd convinced her of that.

At least, as long as it lasts.

He hadn't said more than that, but he hadn't needed to. He'd looked at her as if she'd jabbed him with a straightened coat hanger, a flaming marshmallow at the tip.

He didn't want her to get the wrong idea and think he was interested in something more than a sexual fling. He was afraid she'd expect their relationship to be meaningful and lasting, something that usually called for a church chapel, white lace and wedding vows.

Sheesh. That was the last thing she wanted, especially now that he'd shown his hand.

She was *so* done with sexy bachelors. And the sad thing was, she'd seen right through him the first time she met him. She'd known he was a flirt and a player. But then he'd shown her another side of himself, and against her better judgment, she'd lowered her guard.

And now look at her, crying silent tears in a dumb old tent. She'd rather be anywhere than here.

In fact, if Eddie and Cassie weren't here, she'd...

What? Hike to the county road in the middle of the night and walk home in a huff?

She might be inexperienced when it came to dealing with guys like Adam, but she wasn't stupid enough to wander off in the dark. She'd have to stick it out tonight. And she'd make it through the morning, too, putting on a happy face for the kids—and for Adam—until he dropped them off at her house. Because she'd be darned if she'd let him think that he or that kiss meant a blasted thing to her.

Adam had no idea how long he'd sat at the campfire last night, but he'd remained in his seat well after the flames burned out. When he'd finally turned in, sleep evaded him for what seemed like forever.

Even in the morning, while they all ate cereal and

fruit for breakfast, he did his best to pretend nothing had happened between him and Julie. But that wasn't hard to do. She seemed to be doing the same thing.

Maybe he'd been wrong. She might have actually been tired and hadn't been offended by his knee-jerk response. He sure hoped so, because he didn't want to deal with any apologies or explanations or questions about where they'd go from here.

Because he damn sure wouldn't know what to tell her about the status or the future of their paper marriage. He'd always believed in temporary, rather than lasting. And now she had him questioning his past philosophy.

Once he pulled up in front of her house, she was out of the Bronco before he could shut off the ignition and opening the passenger door. "Come on, kids. Let's take a shower and get ready to go to the ranch."

While the kids piled out of the car, Adam went to the back, opened the rear hatch and withdrew the two backpacks and Julie's tote.

When she took it from him, she cast him a smile. "Camping was fun. Maybe we can do it again sometime."

"Yeah. Sure." He raked his fingers through his hair. "I'll go home and unload the car and come back for you after lunch."

"We'll be ready." Then she headed toward the house.

He ought to be glad she'd made it so easy to slip away without dealing with any questions or suggestions that would have pressured him, but she'd just given *him* the brush-off. And that bothered him more than he wanted to admit.

* * *

After Adam drove Biscuit home and let them both into the house, he went straight to the refrigerator and removed a cold bottle of water. As he took a long, refreshing drink, he noticed the blinking red light on Stan's answering machine, indicating a new message.

Lisa had probably heard the message he'd left her and was calling him back. But he wasn't in a hurry to hear what she had to say. So he took another chug of water, then fed Biscuit before crossing the room and pushing the play button.

He had no idea what to tell her. Maybe that something had come up. Or rather, someone had come up, and he was no longer free to date her. After listening to her message, he'd think of something to say when he returned her call.

But Lisa hadn't called. At least, she hadn't left a message.

The caller had been a telemarketer offering Stan an all-expenses-paid weekend in Las Vegas if he listened to a short time-share sales pitch.

No thanks. Delete.

He'd just turned away from the answering machine, when his cell phone rang. He quickly grabbed it and answered the call. "Hey, Adam! What's up?"

Whenever he didn't recognize a woman's voice, his typical response was to play along at chitchat until a clue to her identity popped up, but he wasn't in the mood for any long, drawn-out games today.

"Who is this?" he asked.

"It's me, Tanya! What are you doing? Are you up

for a night on the town? Or maybe just a quiet evening at my house?"

Even though he kept plenty of stock excuses on hand for invitations like this, he opted to cut to the chase with honesty, just as he would do with Lisa. "Thanks for the offer, Tanya, but I'm going to pass. I'm dating someone now."

"Just *one* somebody? That sounds serious."

He wasn't sure what was going on with him and Julie, but she was the only woman he was interested in dating. "We'll see how things pan out."

"All right," Tanya said. "But if things don't work out, give me a call."

"Yeah, sure." Yet for some reason, he didn't feel like playing the field anymore. And he hoped that things with Julie actually would pan out.

After disconnecting the line, he turned to see Biscuit sitting in the middle of the kitchen floor, watching him with those big brown eyes. "What's the matter, girl? Were you waiting to see if I'd say or do something stupid?"

Her tail swept across the floor.

"Okay," he said, "I'll admit it. Julie is the only woman I'm interested in seeing right now. How about that? Who would have guessed that I'd change my dating MO?"

Biscuit's tail swished faster across the floor. You'd think that they had a genuine inter-species conversation going on, one they both understood.

"I guess you could say that Julie worked a little game-changer magic on me. And apparently, so did the kids."

As Adam reached for his bottle of water and took another swig, Biscuit let out a little woof, which was more of a half bark.

"What's the matter?" he asked.

Biscuit cocked her head to the side.

"Did I forget someone?" Adam shook his head and grinned. "Okay. You've been working on me, too."

Damn. What was happening to him? He was not only talking to a dog, he almost expected her to answer. If he wasn't careful, he'd be referring to Biscuit as a fur baby before he knew it.

Okay, so that's what Biscuit had already become. The kids had really grown on him, too. And in spite of his gut reaction to Julie's comment about their fake marriage last night, he wasn't so sure he liked using words like "paper" or "temporary."

After they took the kids to the Double G to go riding this afternoon and then dropped them off at Kidville, he would take Julie home, where he would apologize for dragging his feet when it came to admitting how he really felt about her.

The pretty music therapist had been strumming away on his heart from the first time he laid eyes on her, and it was time he told her.

Instead of pretending that they were married and living together, he'd ask how she felt about him packing up more of his things and actually moving in with her. If she was willing, he was ready to make their marriage real.

Chapter Eleven

Adam gripped the steering wheel as he drove back to Julie's house. He could have taken Biscuit with him. In fact, the dog whined when he left, but he couldn't very well look after the kids while they rode horses and worry about the dog, too.

He'd packed a suitcase and a couple of boxes and placed them in the back of the Bronco—just in case Julie was willing to let him move in. Surprisingly, the more he thought about it, the better he liked the idea. He glanced at the dash, turned on the radio and adjusted the dial to something upbeat. Then he continued to Julie's house.

When he was only two miles from home, his cell phone rang. His Bronco didn't have Bluetooth capabilities, so he turned on the speaker and answered.

"Adam, it's Martin Chiang."

His friend who worked at the DNA lab. "What's up, Martin?"

"Like you suspected, those kids are definitely siblings—same parents. But we also got a hit on the DNA you supplied. A Jane Doe who was found at the bottom of a canyon about twenty miles from Wexler."

"Murdered?"

"Inconclusive. But now that we have a name— Wanda Cramer—we can investigate further."

"Thanks, Martin. I have a person of interest, who'll probably turn out to be the perp. He's also in custody now. Who's heading the investigation?"

"Tina Singh."

"Thanks. I'll give her a call." Adam had no idea how he'd tell Eddie and Cassie that their mother was dead. But he owed them the truth. He didn't want them thinking that she'd abandoned them.

After calling Tina and telling her Brady Thatcher was a person of interest, he called Julie.

When she answered, he told her the news.

"That's awful."

"Yes, it is. I'll have to tell the kids."

"I know. But maybe you should tell them after Ms. Kincaid's visit."

"Good idea. I'll see you shortly, and we can talk more then." When the call ended, he focused on the road.

Up ahead, the traffic light turned green, which meant he wouldn't need to slow down.

Adam had no more than entered the intersection

when a Ford Mustang slammed into his Bronco, knocking him side to side. Before he had a chance to assess his injuries, the world went dark.

Minutes later—or had it been hours?—a familiar voice called him out of the fog. "Are you okay, buddy?"

Adam, who no longer sat behind the wheel of his Bronco and now lay on the side of the road, opened his eyes. A female paramedic knelt beside him.

The male voice spoke again. Adam squinted at the hazy figure easing closer. "Who...?"

"Pancho, it's me. Bullet."

His old high school buddy. Clay Masters. A Life Flight pilot now. Adam closed his eyes, willing his vision to clear.

"I'm going to fly you to the Brighton Valley Medical Center," Clay said.

The hospital? Damn. That wasn't good. "What... happened?"

"You were in an accident," Clay said. "And it looks like you've got a concussion, not to mention a couple of deep cuts and considerable blood loss."

Adam wiped his palm across his sweaty brow, only to find his hand covered in blood.

His head ached like a son of a gun, and he had a hard time focusing. Still, he reached into his pocket, removed his cell, used his fingerprint to unlock it and handed it to his old high school friend. "Call Julie."

"Who's that?"

"She's..." Adam took a deep breath, then blew it out. "She's my...wife."

"Damn," Clay said. "This isn't good. He's hallucinating."

Adam had no idea who Clay was talking to. A paramedic, he supposed. But he didn't dare open his eyes, since that only made his head hurt worse.

"It's complicated," he told his buddy. "Just give her a call. Her contact info is in my phone. Let her know what happened."

"Will do."

"Tell her to take my dog to her house."

"You have a *dog*? I can't believe it."

"I joined the ranks of people who have fur babies. I'll have to introduce you to Biscuit someday."

Clay laughed. "You've gone whackadoodle."

"Ain't that the truth." Adam grimaced. "Give Julie my address. And tell her where I hide the spare house key."

"Are you sure?" Clay asked. "I mean, you've got a head injury and may not be able to think clearly."

"I've given things a lot more thought than you'll ever know." And it had taken a head injury to shake the truth loose.

"Believe me, buddy, I know what I'm doing."

"Boy, you really do have it bad." Clay chuckled.

"Thanks," Adam said before drifting out again.

Adam's news about the kids' mother had not only surprised and saddened Julie, but it had convinced her that they were still a team, even if their marriage was fake. Instead of regretting she'd agreed to go with him to the ranch, she actually looked forward to it.

He'd said he would see her shortly, but forty-five minutes later, she hadn't seen nor heard from Adam. He'd probably gotten tied up with something or other, so she didn't stress about it until one hour stretched into two.

She reached for her cell phone to give him a call, but before she could get that far, it rang on its own, and she nearly dropped it on the floor. She fumbled to answer it and didn't take time to check the display. "Hello?"

"Julie?"

"Yes…?"

"I'm Clay Masters, a friend of Adam's. He's going to be okay, but he was in a car accident earlier this afternoon and is in the hospital."

"Oh, no." Her knees nearly buckled, and she placed a hand over her chest.

"Like I said, he'll be all right. He's got some lacerations, which the doctor stitched up, and a bad concussion. The doctor wants to keep him a couple of nights because of the head trauma. But it's just a precaution."

Julie's head spun at the thought of Adam's injuries requiring a hospital stay.

"Are you okay?" Clay asked, concern in his tone.

She shook off her stunned reaction. "I'm sorry. It's just that I… Where is he?"

"At the Brighton Valley Medical Center. He wants you to pick up his dog and take care of it for him."

"Of course," Julie said.

"He's sorry that he can't take the kids to the ranch

today and wants you to give them his apologies. He promises he'll reschedule as soon as he can."

"That's all right," she said. "The kids will understand."

"I already contacted Matt, and let him know that Adam will reschedule—possibly next weekend."

"Thanks. I appreciate that. I'll let the kids know and then bring Biscuit here."

"Good. I'll let him know you've got things under control."

Did she?

Her heart was pounding like a bass drum, and the walls seemed to be closing in on her. Just last night she'd been hurt and angry, and this morning she'd been resigned to reality. But now, fear shoved everything else aside.

Clay said Adam would be okay, but she wanted to see for herself. But first things first.

She went to the living room, where the kids were watching television. "Hey, guys. I need to talk to you. Let's turn off the TV, okay?"

As soon as they did as she told them, they turned to her, eyes wide.

"I'm afraid we won't be able to go to the ranch today. Adam was in a car accident."

Both kids gasped, clearly surprised to learn why he was late in returning. Tears welled in Cassie's eyes, and her lip quivered.

"Don't worry," Julie said, trying her best to be upbeat. "He's not hurt badly. And he wanted you to know that he'll take you to the ranch next week."

"Do we have to go back to Kidville now?" Eddie asked.

"Yes, but only because I want to talk to Adam's doctor and see if there are any…special things I need to do for him."

"You promise?" Cassie asked. "He's going to be okay?"

"Yes, I promise." Julie hoped Clay had told her the truth, that Adam would recover. Otherwise…

No, he was going to be fine. And so would she. Learning that he'd been injured, that he might have been killed put everything in perspective.

Last night, she'd been hurt to think that he was looking forward to the annulment, but he really hadn't said that. She'd made something out of nothing. And after a second glass of wine, she hadn't been thinking clearly.

Somehow, she'd set things to right as soon as they had time to talk. She grabbed her purse, locked the house and took the kids to her car. Once she was on the road, she called Kidville and told Jim Hoffman about the accident.

"Oh, no," Jim said. "I'm so sorry to hear that."

"The kids are disappointed, but they understand. I told them we'd reschedule the trip to the ranch." Julie bit down on her lip as a new plan took shape. "Would you mind if I picked them up after I check on Adam? They can spend the night with me again—if that's okay with you."

"I'm sure they'd like that."

"Great." That also meant the kids would be at her house during Ms. Kincaid's visit, although that's not why she wanted to bring them home. She wanted them to all be together while Adam was in the hospital.

After arriving at Kidville Julie took Eddie and Cassie to the office, where the Hoffmans greeted them.

"When you see Adam," Jim said, "give him our best."

"I will."

Once Julie got back in the car, she set her GPS with Adam's address. Just having a purpose put her back in control. And knowing that she was doing something helpful calmed her fears.

Twenty minutes later, she drove down a quiet, tree-shaded lane and parked in front of the address she'd been given. She studied the green stucco house with white trim. She wasn't sure what she'd been expecting. A bachelor pad, she supposed. Not a typical home in a family neighborhood.

She left her car unlocked, figuring it wasn't necessary in this part of town, especially when she wouldn't be inside very long. She'd have to leave Biscuit here for a while, but after she visited Adam in the hospital, she'd return for the dog and take her home.

Using Adam's key, she opened the front door and the dog barked.

"It's only me, sweetie. Don't worry, I'm not a prowler."

As if recognizing her voice, Biscuit rushed to greet her, tail wagging.

"How are you doing?" Julie asked as she bent to give the dog a head rub. "Did you think we forgot you?"

Biscuit wiggled her back end, clearly happy to see someone she knew.

After giving the dog a belly rub, Julie wandered around the living room, noting the masculine decor—a brown leather sofa, dark wood furniture, a bookshelf with novels by Tom Clancy, John Grisham and Stephen King.

She proceeded to the kitchen to give Biscuit fresh water and food. Once the dog's bowls had been replenished, she scanned the cooking area, which didn't appear to be used as such. A coffee maker was the only small appliance on the countertop.

The telephone, a notepad and the old-style answering machine sat on a desk in the corner, its light flashing to indicate Adam had messages. She'd no more than turned away when the telephone rang. After the third ring, the answering machine kicked on.

Julie wouldn't have given the call any thought. Adam could check the message when he got home, until a woman's voice sounded, recording a message.

"Hi, Adam. It's Lisa, returning your call. You asked me to give you a few dates so we can get together for dinner—or whatever." She paused, then let out a little giggle. "Anyway, my flight was canceled, so I'm free on Monday, Thursday and Friday evenings this week. I'm really looking forward to seeing you. You have my number. Give me a call."

Julie's gut clenched, and she returned to the desk, where someone—obviously Adam—had sketched out the name Lisa, followed by a local telephone number.

Apparently, Lisa was returning Adam's call, which sounded as if it had been recent.

The night of the costume party, Adam had mistaken Julie for a woman named Lisa and had whisked her onto the dance floor. Was the caller the same Lisa?

She had to be, and if so, he'd been seeing her all along. The realization crushed her. Her throat tightened to the point it hurt to breathe, and her chest ached. She placed her hand on the edge of the desk to steady herself as her brain took in the unexpected, heart-rattling information. Adam wasn't the kind of guy she'd thought he was.

She'd been right when she'd assessed him as a player. So why had he married her?

For the kids' sake. Just like he'd said all along. He'd never suggested their marriage would ever last. Julie had been the one to hope it could become real.

She'd been charmed, swept off her feet, but he never had anything romantic in mind. Other than a stupid honeymoon, which would be fake, too.

And like a fool, Julie had believed every line he'd given her.

I've learned that it's better to be honest. It makes the story you tell easier to remember.

Yeah, right. And she'd fallen for that line of BS, just like every other one he'd told her. But she wasn't going to fall for his lies again.

Tears welled in her eyes while a seed of anger built inside her like Jack's beanstalk, shoving the pain aside as it continued to grow.

She'd been naive, and she was hurt. But she only

had herself to blame for believing Adam was husband material.

Once Ms. Kincaid approved of the home Julie had created for the kids, Julie would demand that annulment as soon as possible.

Chapter Twelve

Adam stayed in the hospital for three days. He'd expected Julie to visit him on at least one of those, but she never showed up.

He'd been tempted to call her several times, but he hadn't wanted her to think he was needy, even if he'd really wanted to see her. Or at least hear her voice.

She probably hadn't wanted to bother him while he was recuperating. And on top of that, he'd figured that she'd gotten caught up with the social worker's visit. Still, he'd played a big part in getting her house ready, so he'd assumed she would have called or sent him a text to tell him how things had gone.

He hadn't wanted to bother any of his friends by asking one of them for a ride home. Matt was tied up with a lot of rodeo promo this week, and Clay was on duty. So he'd taken an Uber to his house. He'd been tempted to provide her address to the driver instead of his, because he would have preferred to have continued his recovery there. But he wouldn't show up uninvited. Besides, he usually liked to be alone when he wasn't feeling up to speed.

But when he opened the front door and stepped into the living room, silence slammed into him. No barks. No whines.

No Julie.

She'd obviously taken Biscuit to her house, like he'd asked her to. And sure enough, when he entered the kitchen, the dog's water and food bowls were gone. In their place was the key to his house—and a note.

I have the dog.
Julie

That's it? No sentiment whatsoever?

He whipped out his cell and placed the call he'd been wanting to make for days. They might have a fake marriage, but didn't she owe him…something?

An explanation?

A *How are you feeling?*

Physically, better. Thanks for asking. But emotionally, I'm a freaking train wreck.

Rather than act hurt—which he hated to admit he was—when Julie answered, Adam opened the conversation lightheartedly. "Don't pay the ransom, honey. I escaped."

She didn't laugh.

Okay, so she didn't find his attempt at humor funny. He tried another tact. "How'd things go with Ms. Kincaid?"

"Better than expected. She's going to send in her report recommending that Eddie and Cassie live with me."

That was great. But why didn't she sound the least bit happy?

"What's wrong?" he asked.

"Nothing that a quick annulment won't fix."

He stiffened. Where in the hell had that come from?

Okay. He'd been the one to suggest a fake marriage, followed by an annulment. And he'd had every intention of following through. But why so quick? He'd actually gotten used to the idea of spending *more* time with her and the kids. Not less.

But it wasn't just the "quick" part that bothered him. Her response and her tone blew him away. Something was definitely off.

"Don't you think we should hold off on the annulment?" he asked.

"Only until Friday afternoon, the day after Ms. Kincaid officially retires."

Her snappy response knocked him further off stride. "Okay, Julie. Let's back up and start over. I'll be damned if I know why you're so mad. Just lay it on the table so we can deal with it."

"Check your answering machine. And your notepad." At that, she hung up, leaving him stunned. And speechless.

Damn. Had she listened to his recorded messages while she'd been at his house? If so, it served her right for being so damned snoopy.

He strode to Stan's answering machine, the light blinking. He pushed the play button.

"You have one new message and one saved message." Beep.

He knew what the saved message said. And if the other one was new, she hadn't listened to it yet. Or else someone called while she was here and she'd overheard it. That had to be it. And it had really set her off.

"Hi, Adam. It's Lisa, returning your call. You asked me to give you a few dates so we can get together for dinner—or whatever." She giggled, and the sound rolled around his stomach like a rock. "Anyway, my flight was cancelled, so I'm free on Monday, Thursday and Friday evenings next week. I'm really looking forward to getting together. You have my number. Give me a call."

Adam glanced at the notepad, where he'd written her name and number.

Okay, so now he knew why Julie was angry. What should he do about it?

His first inclination was to be grateful that his privacy and independence would stay intact. Instead, loneliness settled over him like a dark rain cloud threatening to drench him to the bone.

He deleted Lisa's message, wishing he hadn't felt the need to return her call in the first place. Then, like he usually did whenever he felt stumped or uneasy, he played Stan's message.

"Hey, Adam. I won't be home tonight. I'm going to take Darlene on the town. That gal might be the one woman in the world who can change this ol' bachelor's mind about commitments.

"Yeah, yeah. You think I'm going soft. Believe it or not, I went the first fifty years of my life without getting roped into marriage, but then I met Darlene, and I actually like the idea of spending the rest of my life with her. Maybe it's time for you to find your Darlene, too."

The answer came to him like a lightning bolt from heaven.

He'd found his Darlene, only to lose her.

What could he do to get her back?

Julie hadn't brought the children to live at her house yet, since the court order had yet to be filed, but when she'd told them where they'd be living, they'd both shrieked with joy.

She'd thought about returning Biscuit to Adam, since he'd been home from the hospital for a couple of days. But he hadn't mentioned anything about the dog, so Julie would keep her until he did.

When she'd last spoken to him, she'd been strong. But with each day that passed, her heart cracked a little bit more. She was convinced she'd done the right thing by shutting him out, but that didn't relieve her pain.

She'd yet to land a full-time job, although the Hoffmans had offered her a part-time position, which she accepted for several reasons. First, she loved everyone at Kidville. Second, she needed an income of some kind. And more important, working only a few days a week would allow her more time to spend with Eddie and Cassie, helping them become adjusted to their new home, their new family situation. The mortgage was nearly paid off, so there was plenty of equity to draw on if she applied for a second.

No worries there.

So why did she find herself plodding through the last two days rather than striding with a happy, confident step?

On Thursday morning, her doorbell rang, drawing her from her musing, which threatened to send her spiraling into depression.

She opened the door and found Adam on the stoop, as gorgeous as ever.

"I need to talk to you," he said.

She had half a notion to slam the door in his face, but she decided to hear him out. She wouldn't let him inside, though.

"I'm sorry for not being up front with you."

She crossed her arms. "So you admit to setting up dates while we were married? I mean, it wasn't a real marriage. I get that. But I expected you to respect me until it ended."

"You expected it to end?" he asked.

"That was the plan." But in truth? No, she hadn't. At least, she'd hoped it wouldn't. She shrugged a single shoulder, as if she didn't care, as if her folded arms weren't holding her broken heart together.

"I'll admit that I enjoyed being single. A lot. And then you walked into my life and turned everything upside down. I haven't seen anyone else since I met you—and I haven't wanted to."

She rolled her eyes and blew out a huff. "Did you listen to your recorded messages?"

"Yes, I did. And I can explain. Before Stan died, he'd tried to set Lisa and me up, but we were both busy and always playing phone tag. I've never even met her in person."

"But you *intend* to."

"No, not anymore. A while back, I returned her call, only to reach her voice mail. I left a message, but then I realized I didn't want to date her or anyone else. I've changed, Julie. Everything's changed since I met you."

She wanted to believe him, but her instincts, which she should have listened to all along, wouldn't let her.

"I'm trying to say that I love you, Julie. You've rocked me to the core. My bachelor days are over." He reached into his pocket and handed her a shiny new key.

"What's this?" She studied it as if she'd never seen anything like it. And in a sense, she never had.

"I made a copy of the key to my house so I could give it to you."

Silence stretched between them as her mind, which had been made up, and her aching heart battled for position. And she tried to make sense of it all.

"I want our marriage to be real," Adam said. "I never

had a real home, a real family. Even though I was happy living with Stan, it wasn't the same thing. So I never knew what I was missing until I met you and the kids."

A whine sounded behind her, and Biscuit eased forward.

"Oops," Adam said. "I didn't mean to leave out the family dog. I want it *all*, Julie. Don't you?"

Yes, she did. The battle inside her ended. Her heart won. Tears welled in her eyes.

"I love you, too," she said, before stepping aside and letting him into her house, into her heart, into her life.

Once inside Julie's house, Adam took her in his arms and kissed her with all the love in his heart. When they finally came up for air, he took a knee, reached into his pocket and pulled out a black velvet jewelry box and gave it to her.

Her fingers trembled as she lifted the lid, and when she saw the sparkling diamond he'd purchased this morning, she gasped.

"Will you marry me?" he asked.

"Actually…" Her smile beamed brighter than the one-carat diamond still in its box. "We're already married."

"Yes, legally. But I want to do it right this time. A proper proposal, an engagement ring, a white dress, a church wedding and a cake, followed by a honeymoon to wherever you've always wanted to go."

Julie removed the ring from the box and slipped it on her finger. She admired it for a moment, then blessed him with a bright-eyed smile that turned him inside out. "Would it be okay if we shook things up a bit?"

At this point, he didn't mind what they did, just as long as she wanted to be his wife, his life partner and his lover.

"What do you suggest we do differently?" he asked.

A sly grin slid across her lips, and her eyes twinkled. "Can we have the honeymoon first? Like…right now?"

Adam got to his feet and wrapped her in his arms once more. "I can't think of anything I'd rather do." Then he placed his mouth on hers as if they'd never been apart, as if there'd never been a question about their feelings for each other.

For a bachelor who'd sworn off marriage, this moment seemed surreal, but kissing Julie, admitting that he loved her, was as real as it got.

They continued to kiss, stroke and caress each other until Julie drew back. "Should we take this to the bedroom?"

Adam was more than ready for that. "You bet we should. But just for the record, I'd make love with you anywhere. Right here on the living room floor, on the kitchen table or even in a tent out at Miller's Creek."

She laughed. "I feel the same way. But a bed might be our best option for our first time."

"As you wish, my lady." Adam reached for her hand and led her to the bedroom. As they stood beside the bed, she reached into the top drawer of her nightstand, opened a new box of condoms, removed one of them and then set it near the lamp.

He wasn't sure if she kept them handy just in case, or if she'd planned for this very moment with him. Either way, he was glad she'd been prepared.

"Good idea." He kissed her again—long and deep—then pulled her hips against a demanding erection. She leaned forward, revealing her own need for him.

As she moved against him, making him even harder, desire surged through him until he thought, if he wasn't careful, he'd implode with the strength of it. Julie must have felt the same way because she ended the kiss and slipped out of her pink T-shirt. When she dropped it to the floor, revealing a lacy white bra, his breath caught. He watched in silence and amazement as she bared her breasts, full and round with dusky pink areolas that begged to be kissed.

He bent and took a nipple in his mouth, suckling first one breast, then loving the other until she swayed and clutched his shoulder. Her nails dug into his skin, creating a sweet pain that aroused him all the more.

He lifted her in his arms and placed her on the bed, her glossy blond hair splayed upon the green pillow sham, her body upon the floral printed comforter. After removing his clothing, he joined her, drawing her beautiful body close to his, skin to skin, heart to heart.

They continued to kiss, taste and stroke each other until they were both drowning in need.

"Wait." She rolled to the side of the bed and reached for the condom, then she offered it to him.

He tore open the packet and rolled it in place. Then, as he hovered over her, she reached for his erection and guided him right where he wanted to be. For the first time in his life, he realized he'd finally found a real *home*.

He entered her, and her body responded his, arching up to meet each of his thrusts. The world stood still. Nothing else mattered but the two of them, what they were doing, the love they were making, the vow of forever.

As Julie reached a peak, she cried out and let go. He shuddered and released along with her in a star-spinning climax that hardly seemed real. But it was. It was as real as it got.

As they lay together in a stunning afterglow, he continued to hold her close, to thank his lucky stars that she'd come into his life.

"You know," he said, "I've had sex plenty of times in the past, but I've never made love before. Not like this. It was amazing. And so are you."

"That makes me happy." She cuddled against him. "Does that mean you'd like to move in with me?"

"Absolutely."

"And you're okay with being a foster dad?"

"Yes," Adam said. "And a real one, too."

She raised up on an elbow, her glossy locks tumbling over her shoulder. "You'd like to have a baby?"

"Sure." He'd like to see her pregnant one day, their child growing inside her. "But I think we should consider adopting Eddie and Cassie."

"I'd love that, Adam."

He tucked a strand of hair behind her ear. "You're

going to be an awesome mother. Not to mention a great wife."

"And you'll be a good father and husband, too."

He sure as hell was going to do everything in his power to prove she hadn't misplaced her faith in him.

He kissed her again, slow and leisurely. Their marriage promised to be a good one. Happy. Loving. And destined to last.

* * * * *

Look for the next book in
USA TODAY *bestselling author Judy Duarte's
Rocking Chair Rodeo miniseries*

*Available June 2019, wherever
Harlequin Special Edition books
and ebooks are sold.*

COMING NEXT MONTH FROM

H HARLEQUIN®

SPECIAL EDITION

Available January 15, 2019

#2671 A SOLDIER'S RETURN
The Women of Brambleberry House • by RaeAnne Thayne
Dr. Eli Sanderson always had a thing for Melissa Fielding, so when he returns home to Cannon Beach, Oregon, he's determined to make a move. After a divorce and her own need to start over, will Melissa's walls be insurmountable?

#2672 HER SECRET TEXAS VALENTINE
The Fortunes of Texas: The Lost Fortunes • by Helen Lacey
When Valene Fortune falls for a seemingly penniless rancher, time—and the truth—will tell if she can love this cowboy for richer as well as poorer!

#2673 THE SERGEANT'S UNEXPECTED FAMILY
Small-Town Sweethearts • by Carrie Nichols
After the end of his Army career, Brody Wilson is content to live out his life caring for abandoned animals on his Vermont farm. But when Mary Carter arrives with his infant nephew, Brody is suddenly thrown into the family life he never thought he could have.

#2674 THE COLONELS' TEXAS PROMISE
American Heroes • by Caro Carson
If they were single by the time they made Lieutenant Colonel, they'd marry. On the day of her promotion, Juliet Grayson is at Evan Stephens's door to ask him to keep his promise. Can he convince a woman who's been burned before to get close to the flame once again?

#2675 HOW TO RESCUE A FAMILY
Furever Yours • by Teri Wilson
Single father Ryan Carter wants just one thing: a new beginning for his grieving son. That means decamping for small-town North Carolina...adopting a rescue dog...even proposing to the gorgeous restaurant manager he can't stop thinking about!

#2676 CLAIMING THE COWBOY'S HEART
Match Made in Haven • by Brenda Harlen
Liam Gilmore is supposed to be focusing on his new inn—but he can't stop thinking about Macy Clayton. He's sure he isn't ready to settle down, but with the single mom of triplets catching his eye, it might be time for Liam to consider forever!

**YOU CAN FIND MORE INFORMATION ON UPCOMING HARLEQUIN® TITLES,
FREE EXCERPTS AND MORE AT WWW.HARLEQUIN.COM.**

HSECNM0119

Get 4 FREE REWARDS!

We'll send you 2 FREE Books plus 2 FREE Mystery Gifts.

Harlequin® Special Edition books feature heroines finding the balance between their work life and personal life on the way to finding true love.

FREE
Value Over
$20

YES! Please send me 2 FREE Harlequin® Special Edition novels and my 2 FREE gifts (gifts are worth about $10 retail). After receiving them, if I don't wish to receive any more books, I can return the shipping statement marked "cancel." If I don't cancel, I will receive 6 brand-new novels every month and be billed just $4.99 per book in the U.S. or $5.74 per book in Canada. That's a savings of at least 12% off the cover price! It's quite a bargain! Shipping and handling is just 50¢ per book in the U.S. and 75¢ per book in Canada.* I understand that accepting the 2 free books and gifts places me under no obligation to buy anything. I can always return a shipment and cancel at any time. The free books and gifts are mine to keep no matter what I decide.

235/335 HDN GMY2

Name (please print)

Address   Apt. #

City   State/Province   Zip/Postal Code

Mail to the Reader Service:
IN U.S.A.: P.O. Box 1341, Buffalo, NY 14240-8531
IN CANADA: P.O. Box 603, Fort Erie, Ontario L2A 5X3

Want to try 2 free books from another series! Call 1-800-873-8635 or visit www.ReaderService.com.

---

*Terms and prices subject to change without notice. Prices do not include sales taxes, which will be charged (if applicable) based on your state or country of residence. Canadian residents will be charged applicable taxes. Offer not valid in Quebec. This offer is limited to one order per household. Books received may not be as shown. Not valid for current subscribers to Harlequin® Special Edition books. All orders subject to approval. Credit or debit balances in a customer's account(s) may be offset by any other outstanding balance owed by or to the customer. Please allow 4 to 6 weeks for delivery. Offer available while quantities last.

Your Privacy—The Reader Service is committed to protecting your privacy. Our Privacy Policy is available online at www.ReaderService.com or upon request from the Reader Service. We make a portion of our mailing list available to reputable third parties that offer products we believe may interest you. If you prefer that we not exchange your name with third parties, or if you wish to clarify or modify your communication preferences, please visit us at www.ReaderService.com/consumerschoice or write to us at Reader Service Preference Service, P.O. Box 9062, Buffalo, NY 14240-9062. Include your complete name and address.

HSE19R

*"Brenda Harlen writes couples with such great
chemistry and characters to root for."*
—**New York Times** *bestselling author Linda Lael Miller*

*The story of committed bachelor Liam Gilmore,
rancher turned innkeeper, and his brand-new manager,
Macy Clayton. She's clearly off-limits, but Liam can't
resist being pulled into her family of adorable triplets!
Is Liam suddenly dreaming of forever after with the
single mom?*

*Read on for a sneak preview of
the next great book in the Match Made in Haven
miniseries,* Claiming the Cowboy's Heart
by Brenda Harlen.

"You kissed me," he reminded her.

"The first time," she acknowledged.

"You kissed me back the second time."

"Has any woman ever not kissed you back?" she
wondered.

"I'm not interested in any other woman right now," he
told her. "I'm only interested in you."

The intensity of his gaze made her belly flutter. "I've
got three kids," she reminded him.

"That's not what's been holding me back."

"What's holding you back?"

"I'm trying to respect our working relationship."

"Yeah, that complicates things," she agreed. Then she finished the wine in her glass and pushed away from the table. "Will you excuse me for a minute? I just want to give my mom a call to check on the kids."

"Of course," he agreed. "But I can't promise the rest of that tart will be there when you get back."

She gave one last, lingering glance at the pastry before she said, "You can finish the tart."

He was tempted by the dessert, but he managed to resist. He didn't know how much longer he could hold out against his attraction to Macy—or if she wanted him to.

Had he crossed a line by flirting with her? She hadn't reacted in a way that suggested she was upset or offended, but she hadn't exactly flirted back, either.

"Is everything okay?" he asked when she returned to the table several minutes later.

She nodded. "I got caught in the middle of an argument."

"With your mom?"

"With myself."

His brows lifted. "Did you win?"

"I hope so," she said.

Then she set an antique key on the table and slid it toward him.

Don't miss
Claiming the Cowboy's Heart *by Brenda Harlen,*
available February 2019 wherever
Harlequin® Special Edition books and ebooks are sold.

www.Harlequin.com

Looking for more satisfying love stories
with community and family at their core?

Check out **Harlequin® Special Edition**
and **Love Inspired®** books!

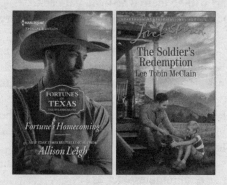

New books available every month!

CONNECT WITH US AT:

Facebook.com/groups/HarlequinConnection

 Facebook.com/HarlequinBooks

Twitter.com/HarlequinBooks

Instagram.com/HarlequinBooks

Pinterest.com/HarlequinBooks

ReaderService.com

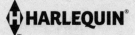

**ROMANCE WHEN
YOU NEED IT**

HFGENRE2018